ALDEN BRIDGE

Also from Joe Cron

Eve of Demons
The Holitaph

ALDEN BRIDGE

JOE CRON

Lardin Press
Everett, Washington

Alden Bridge

Published by Lardin Press

www.lardinpress.com

ISBN-13: 978-0615994291
ISBN-10: 0615994296

For Jill

My one and only.

Chapter 1

I grew up on my eleventh birthday.

Most people move through their childhoods with gradual realizations, maturations, and guidance, and at some point they've grown up. They might feel that way when they're eighteen, or twenty-one, or maybe not until they're thirty-five. For me, it all happened within a span of ten minutes. It happened on my eleventh birthday, when my parents were murdered.

I work on Earth, in an office of the Earth Civilization Outreach Program, or ECOP. It's a comfortable office filled with swarthy wood, plush furniture, and the look and smell of hundreds of old books. There's a desk to one side, but the main part of the room has two stuffed chairs and a cushy, brown couch, all sitting on a huge Oriental rug adorning the hardwood floor. Between those is a long, dark coffee table with picture books, a huge bird talon, and a bowl of mints. Good mints; for some reason no one seems to eat them except me. No one flips through the smooth, glossy pages of the picture books, either, and one of them has some shots of national parks that are truly exceptional. All in all, it's a nice environment for reducing stress.

My job is to reduce stress. I counsel people who have been through traumatic events in their work for ECOP, and I help prepare those whose assignments are about to put them in similar circumstances.

It's important work; not what I would have envisioned for myself, but my background has made me uniquely suited to it, and for the time being, it's nearly as therapeutic for me as for my clients. Eventually, I plan to be in the field again—I feel like I have unfinished business—but for now, this is the right place.

When children get orphaned by murder, it is a terrible, horrible thing. Probably one of the worst things that happen. Maybe losing a child to a murderer is worse. I don't know. Maybe kids are more resilient. Regardless, children losing parents is devastating. When they do, orphans go a lot of different directions. Some have relatives to live with, some go in the system and get assigned to foster homes. Some have nowhere to turn, and live on the streets.

When I got orphaned, there was no one. Literally. Every other person on my planet was dead. There weren't very many, and they all died but me.

Now, I am twenty-five. I've had some time to relate to humans again, and I am participating in society, albeit with a unique perspective. This person I am today knows something of how to deal with difficult situations head-on, and I'm making a difference for my life, both personally and professionally, by using that knowledge. This person has that experience. That person, that child I was, hadn't the slightest idea. I still wonder every day what my life would be like if I had grown up as that child instead of the person he was forced to become.

That child was Alden Waverly.

Like his parents, Alden was tall and slim, with dark hair and skin. His folks looked the part of classic adventurer types—rugged, attractive, and fit—and Alden was following right along on his young path to pioneering.

Alden lived on Cappa Terse, a formerly uninhabited planet on the outskirts of the solar systems colonized by ECOP. The purpose of ECOP was to continuously scout and discover and prepare new planets for human habitation. It was therefore always growing, always reaching out to new worlds beyond anywhere humans had lived before. Such was Cappa Terse.

There were two encampments on Cappa Terse, both established to help determine compatibility and ease of human expansion, with some plain old scientific curiosity thrown in. Curiosity was a strong suit for a ten-year-old kid.

Alden had a lot of strong suits. He was freakishly intelligent. He was also inquisitive, and he loved his life of exploration. He was interested in animals and plants and even rocks. Musicians and sports figures and all that were OK, and he had his favorites, but his real heroes were famous trailblazers, people who had helped bring human civilization to barren worlds. That's what his parents were, and that's what he wanted to be. It was a perfect aspiration to match what seemed an almost unnatural gift for understanding his surroundings and how they worked.

The bigger of the two camps on Cappa Terse was situated in a huge grassland. Almost farther than you could see. The grass was a deep tan color, and tall, almost to Alden's waist. It formed a lush, light brown blanket for miles. There were occasional trees sparsely dotting the terrain; short, broad trees with thick, gnarled wood, and the trees got more dense to the north of the grassland.

The camp supported three families, ten people in all, and there were four buildings to accommodate research, supplies, and living quarters. Strange topographical conditions dominated parts of Cappa Terse, but the grasslands seemed especially conducive to human habitation, and that was the logical area for starting the colonization.

Fifty miles away, at the eastern edge of the grassland, was where some of the topographical oddities began. There was a ravine, thirty feet deep and two hundred feet across, separating the grassland from a large plateau with notably different foliage. On the plateau, there were a few hundred acres of bare, flat rock, and a much larger area of forest, parts of it so thick as to seem like jungle. The strangest part of it was that the ravine extended all the way around the plateau, separating it from the rest of the land. Things grew on the plateau that didn't grow anywhere else on Cappa Terse.

Mostly for that reason, Alden and his parents were on the plateau, in a single building that served as lab, supply shed, and home. It was a nice home.

Alden knew that most people wouldn't consider it a nice home, but to him it was wonderful. His own family, as well as others he knew, was in a more conventional house on Earth before they went off-world. This one on Cappa Terse was wonderful because it was their adventure home. It was what you lived in to be an explorer, a hero. That would never be a hardship to Alden.

They had six rooms. The largest was the living room, and that was mostly because ECOP recognized that people on long-term assignments couldn't simply survive. They needed to have some comfortable breathing room somewhere. The living room was outfitted with light green, short-pile carpeting. It was the only carpeted room, and Alden sometimes preferred the floor to the furniture; he enjoyed the comfortable feel of it. There was a tan couch, dark red stuffed chair, oval-shaped coffee table, and two smaller tables for lamps at either end of the couch.

The beige walls were made of a thin, nanocellulose material, and one of them had a flat video display on it, about three feet wide. They had access to entertainment feeds from ECOP, but they didn't watch very often. Alden enjoyed movies with monsters and explosions, but his parents enjoyed other stuff, mostly. Sometimes, though, he did get to see monsters and explosions.

The rest of the house was plainer, with walls and floors all done in the same nanocellulose material. To someone with more of a decorative sense, it may have been stark and unappealing, but to Alden it was home, and home was wherever their family was, so it was all great. The medium-brown kitchen had a refrigerator, chest freezer, and stove; a UMO, which stood for ultramicrowave oven; a white double sink; a couple of countertops; and a round, yellow table with four chairs. There was their lab, outfitted for two computer tables, some benches for microscopes and other analyzing equipment, and racks for samples and tools. A small bathroom, too, including a toilet, sink, and stand-up shower. The bathroom was elevated, with four steps leading up to it, because the waste and run-off water was collected into sealable containers, like all their garbage was.

They also had a bedroom, with two beds. One wide one for Mom and Dad, and one smaller one for Alden. Sometimes, Alden slept on the couch. He knew why. He didn't get it, but Mom and Dad had explained it to him. It wasn't any problem, anyway; Alden thought it was fun to sleep on the couch.

The last room was their storage room, for all sorts of supplies and things. Mostly food stuff. Canned meats, which Alden liked a lot, and a lot of vegetables, some of which were fine, many of which were tolerated. He did enjoy the canned fruits. There was also flour and sugar, and Alden always loved to see those come out, because it usually meant things like cookies or pie. As difficult as it sometimes was, eating home-fixed meals and dishes was encouraged by ECOP as a way to keep home feeling like home.

For the first year the Waverlys were on Cappa Terse, there were quite a few more people, as they worked to establish the camps and build the buildings. Those people were called the Sec Crew, short for Secondary Crew. The Primary Crew, or Pri Crew, was made up of the people who would stay for the long haul. At least five years, anyway. Some people rotated in or out, but the Pri Crew was essentially the permanent residents.

Once the Sec Crew had left, Alden and his folks were the only ones on the plateau for weeks at a time. If there were any social or other developmental considerations that Alden was missing out on, he was oblivious. To him, this was a constant adventure. He'd been on Earth until he was seven, the age that ECOP approved families to go mobile, so he had some exposure to classrooms and playmates and such. His family went through a couple years of off-world orientation and training, at which they excelled, then they got the assignment to Cappa Terse.

Alden never had any fears about leaving all that Earth stuff behind to go wherever his parents were going, and he never had second thoughts about how life could be different. He was too young for any of that. Alden loved his folks and everything they did, and they showed Alden a magical childhood. They were well into their second year as the Pri Crew, and his parents were passionate about the mission and about enjoying it.

Not that they were simply abandoned to their work. There was a supply ship from ECOP once a month, which actually seemed fairly often. Some months they were a little bit surprised to realize supply day was already coming up again. There was also ground transportation on the planet by way of a pair of four-person, all-terrain buggies for the Pri Crew to use for exploration and visits between the camps. They were something in between a dune vehicle and a real car, yellow with slightly oversized tires, a metal roof, and glass windows. All in all, it never seemed like they were apart from humanity. Not at first.

One of the critical things built by the Sec Crew was the bridge. ECOP wanted to know more about the unique nature of the plateau, but didn't want any crew there to be totally reliant on supply ships to move around. They built a bridge between the plateau and the grasslands, wide enough for a buggy. It was designed to be dismantled, eventually, since the uniqueness of the plateau was predicated on its physical separation from its surroundings, and ECOP did not want to jeopardize that in any long-term colonization. For the time being, though, it was an important lifeline.

Because the bridge was only meant to be in place a short time, and one of the Sec Crew, Basil, was working his last assignment—a short-timer—they joked that it would be appropriate to name the bridge after him, so at each end of it, they put up wooden signs just to the right of the bridge entry, with crude, hand-painted letters reading "Basil Bridge."

The bridge was one of Alden's favorite parts of life on Cappa Terse. He wasn't supposed to go on it, because it was not made for pedestrian safety, but of course that did little to keep him away. He loved to look into the ravine and watch the stream that ran down the middle of it, even though much of the stream was overgrown with foliage and couldn't be seen. The Sec Crew cleared away the dense brush where the bridge was being built, so the stream could be seen directly under it and for maybe thirty feet on either side. The stream was not deep and only ten feet across, but running water was fascinating in the way that only running water is.

The stream wasn't the only water around. In fact, one of the oddities of the plateau was that water was readily available from a large spring deep in the forest, creating a pond that ran off in another stream through the back of the forest to a waterfall into the ravine. That was another wonderful place, but it was much, much farther from their camp building than the bridge was. There was a crude path cleared through the densest parts of the forest jungle along the creek from the pond to the waterfall, but it took all of a long day to get there and back on foot, and Alden never had nearly enough time to make that trip without his parents needing him. He tried it, of course, and he remembered that day very plainly. His mom and dad had never been that mad.

Water was important to their camp and to any consideration of humans living there in the future. The open area of rock at the southern end of the plateau was open because nothing could grow there, but closer to the edge of the forest, there was soil, and they had a garden to help with a few food supplies and to study how well things could grow.

Part of setting up the camp was creating a water line from the spring pond. They had a huge, solar-powered pump nearly as tall as Alden, feeding fresh water through a pipe for thousands of feet through the forest. There was a valve to divert water to irrigation ruts between the garden crop lines, and the main line continued to their camp building. There was already foliage growing in the soil—small, thick-leaved plants that had to be cleared away for the crops—meaning there was enough natural water for something to grow, but actual farming was different. They needed the irrigation system to guarantee the crops would make it through the year.

Alden appreciated the irrigation system, because the water came blasting out of a big, short tube that was chest-high for Alden, and after long weeks of sun, nothing was like standing in front of the blast. It would knock him over into the mud, then he would just wash the mud off in the heavy stream and start over.

The natural water came during a rainy season. Days on Cappa Terse were very close to a day on Earth—less than eighteen minutes longer—and the year on Cappa Terse was only about a month longer than a year on Earth. Since more of the year was very dry, ECOP and the Pri Crew agreed to chart the year with an extra month of twenty-six days between June and July. The man who discovered Cappa Terse was fond of his Italian heritage, so the month was named Arido, a word from Italian—and other languages, giving it broader recognition—for "arid." Earlier in the year, around March and April, was the rain.

The rain was heavy, and with some scattered showers in the fall, it served to keep all the plant life going. The plant life was interesting.

The most prominent of the plants were the trees that made up most of the plateau forest. Alden couldn't pronounce the scientific name assigned by the Pri Crew, but everyone referred to them as brushtops. They grew thirty to forty feet tall and about two feet in diameter, with no lower branches. All the leaves came from a crown that billowed with long, weeping vines drooping down more than half-way to the ground. On still days, they created an eerie canopy of sagging foliage, and on breezy days they rustled with sweeping patterns that seemed to show exactly how the air was moving. It was like you could see the wind. The rustling released a sweet, floral scent that filled the forest, especially as the breezes died down and the scent settled into the still air below.

The first few hundred acres of forest closest to the open rock were not as dense with lower vegetation as the deeper, back portions where the spring pond and stream were. Alden was free to roam the trees, and it was a marvelous playground.

The bark of the brushtops was a dark purple-grey, and it was thin. The trunks were soft and very fleshy, retaining as much water from the rainy season as they could store, but after they died or fell for whatever reason, the wood became quite hard. While moist, the wood was somewhat malleable; they had discovered that if a newly fallen tree had weight on it, such as a second tree falling on top, it was soft enough to flatten quite a bit before it hardened. As a potential crop, this would make it very easy to use, as it could be gently bent into any crude shape when it was harvested, then cured into a rigid form. There was a lot to learn about these trees before farming could be done, as they were one of the plants that only grew on the plateau, and they would not be allowed to be threatened. Once understood, though, they showed promise as a valuable potential resource.

Animal life on Cappa Terse was limited, especially on the plateau, where there were no crawling or walking animals at all. Only birds and some flying insects. The birds were primarily two types. There were blue birds about the size of a raven, and smaller ones whose heads were a deep red, with brown bodies. The insects were neither plentiful nor aggressive, though some appeared intimidating, like dragonflies. None of them bit or stung by nature, so cohabitation was stress-free. All the land animals were in the grassland and beyond, covering the rest of the planet. Some were not terribly friendly, but that was part of the charter of the larger camp, the Grass Camp. They were evaluating animal life, among other things. From the Plateau Camp, Alden and his parents were focused on plants.

There was lots of learning time for Alden. Some technologies were available for communicating with ECOP, including Leap-Distance Frequency radio, or LDF, which was how they coordinated necessary supplies for the monthly ship visits. They had video capabilities and back-up audio radios, and the video allowed Alden to connect with classes held at ECOP for the various thousands of off-world families. That was only a couple of times a week, though, and the bulk of Alden's studies came through old-fashioned books and projects and accompanying his mom or dad through whatever they were doing.

Studying with Mom was usually indoor stuff: book learning, scheduled lessons, and Alden's favorite indoor activity, lab analysis of the plants. Alden was fascinated by seeing the stuff of the real universe, looking through microscopes and dabbing with chemicals and such. Dad did his share of that with them, but Dad did more of the outdoor things—the gardening and the trips into the forest—and Alden loved the outdoor learning. With an atmosphere so similar to Earth's, the daytime sky was a familiar blue, though a tiny bit deeper. They weren't outside after dark much, but that was interesting learning, also, as Cappa Terse had two moons, in a similar plane of orbit, but in opposite directions. Like Earth, the lunar cycles appeared with a sliver of new moon on to one that was bright and full. Many nights, only one was visible in the early dusk, but sometimes both. About every eight months, both were full at the same time, and that was too spectacular to miss. Day or night, Alden's time outdoors was very special to him. That was a good thing, for a variety of reasons.

When it was play time, there was no finer place for Alden than his rock cave. Their camp building was situated on the bare rock, roughly a thousand feet from the bridge and ravine to the west, and perhaps five hundred feet from the garden and the thin edge of the forest to the north. Farther east from the building, another fifty yards away from the bridge, was a circular hole in the open rock.

The hole was only about four feet across, and below it was a small cavern, as big as a one-car garage. At the far end, it reduced to a hole too small to crawl into, that must have continued out to either the ravine or a larger underground cavern, because rainwater drained out instead of pooling. Once they had determined nothing was living in it, they dropped a wooden ladder and it became Alden's realm. He had a lamp, a couple of logs, a notebook, a water jug—essential play cave stuff. The wonders of countless galaxies were discovered, conquered, or explored in that small cavern.

Alden's world of learning, playing, and dreaming beyond all possibilities was boundless, yet far too small to encompass what reality could include.

Chapter 2

Alden's eleventh birthday had been a marvelous day. It was late May, the rains had been gone for weeks, and he was enjoying his time both indoors and out. He was in his typical khaki shorts, tennis shoes, and oversized, green T-shirt with an image of one of his favorite game characters, Thalok, a fictitious warrior. The supply ship was there three days earlier, and the pilot gave Alden a new plant for the garden. He waited until his birthday morning to plant it, which was done with some appropriate ceremony.

Seven members of the Pri Crew from the Grass Camp came over to celebrate with him. Their birthday gift was simple, but effective: photographs of a number of the animals they had been able to track down in the grassland, and all the way to the edges of the far bush territory.

There were birds, but Alden saw birds on the plateau. He was more interested in the crawlers. He saw lizards and rodents, and some of the dangerous animals, like some crabby-looking things with poisonous pincers. They'd also found a couple of the larger species, such as a hairless, hunting cat that wasn't as big as a lion or tiger but looked freakishly evil; and a huge, thick, hooved animal resembling a rhinoceros, but without the horn, and sporting a huge, bony collar around its neck. It was a blurry photo, and at a good distance, but it proved they were out there. Alden had read about some of those animals already, but he loved seeing the pictures from the Grass Camp safari trips.

Along with the pictures were many, many stories. Twelve-year-old Randy showed Alden the two small, round scars on his foot where one of the crabs pinched him. He got a very high fever and was sick for two weeks. They saw an enormous bird—much larger than anything nesting on the plateau—swoop down and pick up one of the cats. Every photo had a tale to tell. It was a life of long, tedious days, but it was also one of wonder.

At mid-afternoon, the Grass Camp crew left, and Dad had to go with them to drive one of the buggies back. There were no studies that day, being Alden's birthday, and he went out to his play cave until Dad came home for dinner.

After an hour, Alden went to the house so his mom knew where he was. That was the arrangement, as a result of one or two ill-advised extended hikes into the deep forest. There was more business waiting in the cave—important play stuff—and he hurried back. At the end of a second hour, the sun was just getting low enough that Alden needed more light to see things. As he sat on a log and picked up his lantern, he heard a familiar sound. It was the tires of a buggy coming over the bridge. Dad was home!

There was another sound, too, that was almost familiar, but not quite. It was like the noise the supply ship made. But the supply ship was just there three days earlier. As he stood and put his lantern down, the sound was coming closer.

Then, two blasting, rollicking explosions pounded Alden's ears. He fell over in the cave, from the sheer surprise. A wave of red light passed over him, and the ship sound got louder, then quickly faded away.

Alden was breathing very quickly and his hands were shaking as he scrambled as fast as he could up the ladder and out of the cave.

The sight before him was utterly unbelievable. He nearly fell back into the hole, but was struck by the urge to run. The camp building was obliterated. The walls were rubble, and smoke and tall fires rose from the destroyed remains. Even out by his cave, the ground was strewn here and there with scattered items from home, blown in all directions.

"Mom!" screamed Alden at the top of his lungs, amid short breaths and panicked footsteps.

"MOM!"

He sprinted up to the building, or as close to it as he could get.

"MOM!"

There were snaps and hisses and faint clangs from within the roaring flames, but nothing was the voice of his mother. He ran around to another side of the crumbled walls, peering into the inferno. This time his voice cracked.

"Mom?"

He paused and coughed from the smoke. Nothing in the building was moving.

His dad should be there. Yes—he knew he heard the tires on the bridge.

"DAD!" he yelled as he bolted off toward the bridge.

He didn't see the buggy anywhere, and it was only a few steps before he could see smoke billowing up from the ravine. He ran, and called for his father the entire distance. He couldn't allow himself to acknowledge thoughts about what might have happened. Only about running as fast as he could.

When he got to the bridge, it was gone. Only a small chunk of it remained on his side, and across the ravine, it was blown away to the bare rock. He stood at the edge and looked down.

"Dad!" he called. The ravine was some thirty feet deep, and at the bottom, lying in the thick brush, was a mass of twisted, smoldering metal.

Alden remembered that there was a metal ladder at their end, right next to the rock face. The Sec Crew used it during construction, and left it there in case the Pri Crew ever needed to get into the ravine. It was still in place. Ignoring whether or not it was firm or safe, Alden quickly began climbing down.

On the way down the ladder, Alden began to have a concept of what might be happening. He dismissed it immediately. That could not be true.

He reached the bottom, and hurried over to the edge of the brush. The buggy landed a short distance into the thicket, and Alden couldn't see very well.

"Dad!" he called again. No answer.

He pulled at some of the branches in a frenzy. They were very thick, and rough. He pulled harder. Harder, bending and twisting. He got one to break. There were dozens. He decided to climb through. The branches were dense, but not like a canopy he could just climb across. He found a place for his foot. Then another, holding higher branches. His foot slipped, and he fell between the bushes, scraping his leg. He pulled himself up. He held tighter as he placed his foot again. He found another foothold. He slipped again. He struggled and pulled some more and finally got close enough to lunge forward with his body prone and resting on branches, and he could see inside the buggy.

Alden was stunned in a way he could not have fathomed. He closed his eyes immediately, but would never be able to not see it. His father was not going to answer him.

Alden stayed suspended in the thick branches of the brush for many minutes. This could not be true. Could not be. Could not be.

Alden opened his eyes to the early glow of morning. He was a little shocked to feel like his nightmare was still happening in his mind, and his body twitched from the startling realization that he was outdoors. With that movement, he slipped a little down into the brush where he was suspended in the web of foliage. His next thought was that he was in deep trouble. He had done something, fallen asleep, and spent the entire night outdoors, and there was going to be serious punishment.

Then it all came flooding back.

Almost, anyway. His mind seemed to slam the doors on the flood, as if he could see the flood coming and knew what was in it, and closed a huge door that kept it out. Even so, he knew without thinking that he wanted to get away from the mangled buggy next to him without looking inside.

He moved his body a little and settled a bit farther down into the brush. Something scraped his arm, and it stung a little more than it should. He looked down and saw three small welts on his left forearm. Bites. Must have happened while he was sleeping. He'd learned enough to know that flying bugs don't often bite more than once, and if they did they wouldn't bite in a line.

There were crawling things in the brush of the ravine.

Alden surmised that casual movement was probably bad. He was going to need to muster up determination and energy something similar to what he'd spent getting into his position in order to get out of it. He took a breath and began grabbing and pulling and finding places for his feet to push. He slipped a couple more times, but eventually tumbled out of the thick brush and into the cleared area.

This was the first he had noticed that the bridge frame was laying all around the ravine in metal pretzels. For the moment, he ignored that. Another instinct hit him out of the blue.

"Dad! Mom!"

He instantly realized Mom could be OK. She could have crawled out of the burning wreckage of their house while he was in the ravine. He raced to the ladder and scrambled back up.

Even though the bridge was missing and he couldn't help but be aware of that all the way up the ladder, Alden turned when he got to the top and looked out over the empty ravine. The same wave of terror came over him as it had when he arrived at that scene from the end of a dead sprint. He couldn't think about that again.

Alden turned and ran straight toward the rubble of the camp building. The stillness of the morning belied the fresh panic in Alden as he called out for Mom. She would come running out to him, and this would be fine. A few hundred feet away from the crumbling foundation, he froze in his tracks. A thought occurred to him. He might actually find his mother. If that was going to be anything like finding Dad, he couldn't allow that to happen.

At that moment, his entire demeanor transformed.

Keeping a safe distance of about a hundred feet, Alden walked calmly around the building and continued on to the entrance of his cave. He climbed down in, sat on a log, picked up his notebook and pen, and began drawing. He often drew sketches; they were crude, but they were his. They were both the inspiration for and product of his imagination. This time, all he drew were jagged, pointed lines, in a heavy hand. On calm days like this, he could hear Mom calling from home, and he was sure she'd be after him any minute. Breakfast was the most important meal of the day, and he shouldn't be in his cave that early. He was surely in trouble now. Alden wanted very much to be in trouble with his parents.

There was no way to make sense of the confluence of knowledge and denial that swirled in Alden's mind, and he shut it all out. After a few minutes, though, it occurred to him that his friends from the Grass Camp would be checking on him. They must have heard the explosions. He wouldn't want to miss them.

He climbed back out of the cave, walked all the way back near the entrance to the bridge, and sat on a rock. The ground there was a gently flowing terrain of small layers and levels of bare, light-brown rock, but there were also plenty of loose, flat rocks sitting on the ground, and Alden chose one as a bench.

He sat and stared across the ravine.

Any minute now, the Grass Camp folks would pull up over there and things would be OK.

All he had to do was wait.

Any minute now.

He sure was hungry and thirsty.

It didn't really take very long for Alden to realize how foolish this was. He'd known it the whole time, of course. He'd known better than to be genuinely optimistic, but before that moment was unwilling to choose a time to recognize it. Now was that time. This was the time he began to cry.

Once it started, it took over. He cried hard, sitting on

the rock, and screamed with all his might. He crumpled down off the rock onto his hands and knees, crying. His fingers clenched into fists and he cried and pounded the ground. He took deep breaths and cried them out until his lungs were completely empty and no noise came out. He rolled around, he screamed, he convulsed, and cried some more. He got up and ran, and stopped to throw his arms out and yell. There was nothing his body could do to express the pain. It was overwhelming, in the truest, deepest, sharpest sense possible.

He ran to the ravine to throw himself in, then stopped at the edge for no reason. There wasn't a single reason not to jump, but he didn't. Maybe he wasn't ready to die. Maybe he just wasn't finished crying, and when he was, he'd be ready to die. Maybe he was afraid he wouldn't die—he would just fall to a crippling injury, lying there unable to move forever until he starved to death. There was no reason; he just didn't do it.

Instead, he dropped to his knees and began crying more heavily. Nothing was right. Absolutely nothing. Nothing in his life was right, and even dying wasn't right. There was no escape, nowhere to turn away from things that were intensely not right. He sobbed and sobbed right there at the edge of the ravine until he was completely breathless, and he stopped. He still wanted to cry; everything was just as horrific as it had been a few seconds earlier, but just as he had stopped from jumping into the ravine, he simply stopped crying, and couldn't comprehend it.

Then, in a moment he would never be able to explain, Alden decided not to die that day. For no reason. There was no reason to do anything at all. He just made up his mind not to die that day.

Alden stood, turned, and walked toward the rubble of his house. About half-way there, he began to notice there were odds and ends from their home scattered about. He'd walked through them several times already, and saw them, but hadn't noticed. A lot of it was charred chunks of walls and shards of glass and the like. A little closer to the building, he saw a hammer. He picked it up and thought he should probably keep it, then realized he had nowhere to put it, and dropped it again.

When he got closer, he moved around it at his safe distance, to get to the back, where he could see there were several large things lying on the ground. It looked like all the kitchen appliances and such were blasted straight out the back of the house. They were quite a ways from the foundation now.

The refrigerator was on its back, the exterior surfaces warped and deformed from heat. Alden was in a strangely detached frame of mind. It seemed as almost a given that this would be the condition the appliances were in, and he thought nothing of it. It was the refrigerator, and it had stuff in it he ate and drank. Plain and simple.

Alden went up to it and tried to tug up on the door, but couldn't budge it. The rubber seal had melted and fused the door closed, and the hinges were out of alignment. He climbed up to stand on the freezer portion and yank up from there, and finally the seal ripped apart and the door creaked open. It was a mess. This was of no consequence to Alden. Of course it was a mess. The thing had probably rolled over four or five times on its way here. Some things had broken, and there was cherry pie everywhere, but the explosion had happened so quickly that it was all still chilly inside.

What Alden wanted most was still there for him: fourteen unruptured plastic bottles of water. The water supply from the spring pond was fresh and drinkable, but they kept plenty of bottled water around as well, and Alden wanted an easy container. He sat down on the freezer door with his legs inside the refrigerator compartment, grabbed a bottle, wiped some stuff off it with his shirt, then opened it and took several huge gulps. He found a couple globs of pie that weren't too mangled to get a hold of, and quickly gobbled those down. Cherry pie was his favorite. Peach and apple were both really good, but cherry had a tartness he liked best. At the moment, his point of view was such that he was just happy to be eating cherry pie, not sad that much of it was splattered and beyond retrieving, or annoyed by acknowledging that his life was utterly destroyed and that everyone and everything he knew or loved was completely obliterated. In this instant, the taste of cherry pie gave him an excuse to ignore everything else.

Alden wasn't really thinking much about anything beyond what was right in front of him. See pie, eat pie. Here is water. Drink water. He had no thoughts for the scope of his situation. That was all too much. As long as he wasn't dead, he was accomplishing his goal for that day. That was the only real decision he had made. Don't die.

He grabbed a couple of bottles of water, managed to shove the door closed again, and ambled off toward his cave. His cave was the only place that was the same. As he walked, he started to consider his circumstance like a game. He'd already found the precious water he needed. There would be other things to find, things to keep him alive that day. The cave would help. The cave would be a good place to make a plan for how to play this game and get home again.

If only he knew what home was going to be.

Chapter 3

Alden's cave was not the same. It hadn't been damaged in any way; it just wasn't the same. He sat and thought, but he was unable to let his mind go anywhere. The game plan idea was not forming in any way. Even his imagination had nowhere to go. Just a short time ago, even the last time he was in his cave, he was unable to consider his situation, and now he was unable to consider anything else.

Strangely, though, he couldn't actually organize any thoughts into things like what he should do. That was more cohesive than he could muster. It was as if he thought he should think about what to do, but didn't know how. He was lost in an inescapable storm of images in his mind.

A couple of times, his thoughts reached a point where it suddenly seemed too outrageous to be true.

Why was he thinking about this? It couldn't have actually happened. He climbed the cave ladder far enough to stick his head out the hole and see the devastation, then climb back down and start thinking again.

This went on for two hours, until he broke down again under the weight of how unfair this was, and had another crying spell. Deep, heavy, violent crying, and again it left him spent.

When it was finished, he had a moment of realization. It was basic, but essential. Step One. Nothing was going to change unless he did something. Part of him had been denying this so far, clinging to a desperate hope that something outside of him would change to simply save him. He would wake up, or Mom and Dad would just come walking around and tell him this was all a crazy mistake, or someone else would show up and take him away to a safe, comfortable place.

He remembered the moment when he decided not to die today, the moment by the edge of the ravine. That moment was similar in some ways to this one, but beneath that other one was still denial in the sense that, even if he was not going to die, he was not necessarily responsible for everything it would take to stay alive. This time, there was a clear acceptance of the responsibility to take care of himself. In that acceptance was the simultaneous acknowledgement that his parents were gone. If something happened that showed him this was all just a horrible illusion—something like waking up—he would gladly accept that. Until then, this was reality. He would never see his parents again, would likely never see anyone from the Grass Camp again, and would need to survive solely by his own actions until the next supply ship visit, twenty-seven days away.

There was some clarity in this moment. In particular, he was able to think more directly about his next actions. Oddly, within the horror of his loss, this simple concept gave him a measure of relief. He felt like something had been lifted from him, just by being able to think about what to do next.

He was ready to consider how to eat and drink. Not in the fairly delirious way he had gotten the water and pie from the refrigerator, but in a more planned way that would keep him alive until the supply ship visit.

Alden climbed out of the cave and stood, looking out over the debris. The breezes were very light that day, and the sun was still a couple hours from midday. It would be a pretty good day to see what was lying around and could be saved or used. He thought of the game concept again, being a character searching for survival supplies to reach the next game level. That appealed to him, and gave him a place to put his brain that was somewhere besides constant terror and sadness.

He began to walk, realizing he didn't know quite where yet. Walking was OK, though, and he'd think of a plan while he looked around.

Alden saw his legs while he was walking, of course, and they made him stop and look more closely. He was filthy. It struck him as very odd that he had actually gotten all the way to this point without giving any consideration whatsoever to what condition he was in. Alden made a mental note to himself about how interesting that was in the way his mind worked. He was fond of considering those kinds of things.

In any event, he was a mess. His legs had numerous scrapes and dried drippings of blood. His clothes were a hodge-podge of dirt, snot, and cherry pie. He remembered the bites on his arm, and looked at those, but they were still small. They weren't going to turn into anything dangerous.

In light of this, Alden changed his immediate plan to washing off somehow. Besides food and drink, he quickly became aware this was his first challenge in how to deal with no house. Then, he started thinking of the rest of it. Besides washing, there were sleeping and bathroom considerations. And besides washing himself, there were his clothes. And did he even have any clothes besides what he was wearing?

Alden became slightly panicked about this, and the leading edge of another crying fit started to come over him, but from nowhere he remembered how his dad had spoken with him about solving problems. All kinds of problems, from getting the lid off a jar to understanding the environment of a planet. Everything is about your next step. Focus on one thing at a time. No matter what the problem is, even if fixing it takes a million steps, the only way to take the millionth step is to take the one in front of you. So, all you ever really need to know is the next step.

For Alden, right now, the next step was how to clean himself off. Everything else could wait until he was done with that.

Once that was clear, how to do it was, too. The irrigation tube was easy, and he'd washed himself off in that many times. It was quite a ways off—about a quarter of a mile to the garden from his cave—but if they had gotten used to anything on Cappa Terse, it was walking. It was about the same distance to the ravine from the house, but they usually covered that on a buggy. Not anymore. Every trip Alden had made back and forth since the explosions, and every trip he would make anywhere from now on, would be on foot.

When he got to the irrigation tube valve, he grabbed the valve like either he or Mom or Dad had done in the past. It was a big, red, metal bar that stuck out sideways from the pipe. Sideways was off. Turning it the same direction as the tube was on. With some effort, he got it turned on, and the water came out, but not nearly in the kind of blast he was used to. He had no idea why that would be, but he went ahead and got himself into the flow of water and started rubbing with his hands to get the easy stuff off. There were stains, especially blood and cherry, that weren't going away. Alden figured they need soap, and he also figured he wouldn't have any, but that didn't bother him. Cherry stains on his shorts were the least of his worries. He knew his mom wouldn't be very happy, but then remembered she would never see them. The crying wave came quickly, but he shut it down. There was a water problem.

He had no idea how the water pipe attached to anything at the house, but it didn't take long for Alden to realize that if the house wasn't there anymore, the water connection wasn't, either, and that could be causing this. He decided to walk next to the water pipe toward the house and see what he could see. He was soaking wet in all his clothes, but the day was warm, as most days were, and he'd been soaking wet before. He'd dry off quickly in the sun.

For the whole trip toward the house, he couldn't see any leaking or anything wrong with the water pipe. Then, he was getting very close to the building. Uncomfortably close. Regardless of any realizations or whatever problem-solving mode he was in, seeing Mom was still utterly out of the question. He decided to go around the house at his safe distance and see whatever he might be able to without getting closer.

Sure enough, when he approached the back side, back by the appliances, there was a strong stream of water flowing out of the foundation of the house and across the ground, making its way into the distance. That was weird. It had to have been there the whole time. He must have stepped right in it when he came by here earlier to the refrigerator. Clearly, his mind was somewhere else.

Alden thought about following the stream to see where it went. He presumed that it eventually dumped into the ravine, and he was curious about where. He wanted to see the little waterfall. That would be cool. It was more important to fix this, though. Alden had a feeling this would not be the last cool thing he would miss in favor of what was necessary.

As he thought about the water, two things came to mind. One was that there was another valve on the pipe to the house, right next to the one on the irrigation tube. They never used the one to the house, but it was there in case it ever had to be shut off. Today, it had to be, and that's what brought up the second thing. This water had been pumping off like this for a long time, now, and the spring pond might be going dry. Mom and Dad had always said they didn't want the irrigation tube to be on too long because they didn't want the level in the spring pond to go down, and now the stream gushing out the back of the house was a lot of water.

Even though it had been hours and hours that the water pipe had been flowing freely, this suddenly seemed urgent to Alden. If the spring pond was low, things in the forest would not get water from the forest stream, and that was not good. He ran most of the way back to the pipe valves. The house valve had never been moved, and it was stuck. Alden kept shoving on it, and eventually he got it to budge. After that, it was easier to close the rest of the way.

Alden felt like he had gotten an important thing done, and he heaved a sigh of relief. This was good for him. This was his first accomplishment, the first unexpected problem, and he solved it. He was proud of himself.

Now, he was curious about what the spring pond looked like. He wanted to see if it would go down like Mom and Dad said. There were problems with this, though. He was thirsty again. He still had bottled water in his cave, and there was more in the refrigerator, but those were a quarter-mile away. The spring pond was the other direction, into the forest, but a long way in. Farther than his cave. If he took off into the forest from here, there would be nothing to drink for a couple of hours. Also, there would be nothing on his head.

Sun was an issue on Cappa Terse. Most days of the year, there were very few clouds. The rainy season was the exact opposite, but that was only two months out of thirteen. In the fall, there were a few more showers, but only interspersed with sunny days. Alden and his folks spent a lot of time outside, and Alden had been coached well on how to avoid sun problems. Mostly, sunscreen and hats.

Alden did wear hats often. Sunburn on his neck and face was no fun. As for his arms and legs, he was less diligent about sunscreen, and he had a deep tan. His arms and legs didn't burn anymore. Mom and Dad scolded him about that, because there were health issues, but it never sank in.

That day, Alden was never happier that he was not going to have to worry about arm and leg sunscreen, but he was concerned about his head. That could be a problem later on.

In the end, Alden decided the forest would block a lot of sun, he could do without water for a while, and if the spring pond wasn't being drained anymore, this was the lowest it would ever be. He wanted to see it.

Traveling next to the water pipe was the easiest way through the forest. They had made sure there was a path next to it, in case anything needed repair. For the first half-hour, there wasn't much undergrowth, anyway. Some downed trees were scattered here and there through the woods, and the ground had a thick blanket of old, fallen vines from the brushtops, but there wasn't a lot of low growth.

After a while, it got thicker. First were ferns and some low bushes with tiny, round leaves. Past the spring pond were plants that grew with long, broad leaves right out of the ground, bunched together. Further into the woods, the brushtops got slightly thinner, and the ground plants took over. There was a combination of things with long, fleshy stalks and huge leaves, growing between stout bushes with dark, spade-shaped leaves. It was all very dense and taller than Alden. The path along the stream was the only way through that stuff.

The spring pond was as deep into the forest as Alden was allowed to go on a normal day, keeping him able to get back to the house and check in with Mom and Dad within a reasonable time period. Earlier in their stay on Cappa Terse, Alden explored deeper when his curiosity drove him there, and that was how the check-in policy got instituted. Once, he got all the way to the deep waterfall, where the stream from the spring pool empties into the ravine. That was a fabulous place. He'd been there with his parents, too, but once he went on his own. On his way back, Mom and Dad met up with him in a terrible panic, calling and screaming for him. Alden was confused by all the crying and smiles combined with anger and punishment, but he'd take that confusion all day every day right about now.

Chapter 4

As Alden approached the area of the spring pond, he came upon their water pump, which was churning away. It was OK to be running all the time, since that's how it always was. It had some kind of system in it for knowing when there was no water flowing out the other end, and not build up pressure and explode or burn up. Still, Alden wasn't sure how he was going to use the water, and considered figuring out how to shut it off. In another moment, he realized if he couldn't get it back on again, he'd be in trouble. Also, the irrigation tube would be handy, as it already had. He decided to leave it alone.

The pump was only a short distance from the spring pond, and when Alden reached it, he was shocked. The pond was only fifty feet across, but it was quite deep, and the water level was way down, much farther into the pool than Alden's height. As would happen many, many times, his first thought was to get Mom and Dad out there to see it. He quickly reminded himself that wasn't going to happen, but in a strange bit of denial, his next thought was that he'd tell them later. His mind wasn't ready to come completely to grips with the idea that discoveries like this were only for him now.

He laid down on his stomach, resting his head on his arms in front of him at the edge of the pond crater, and studied it. The water was extremely clean and clear, so they'd always been able to see deeply into it, but the exposed pond walls were more clear now, and it was fascinating. For the first five feet or so—about as tall as Alden—the ground was medium-brown dirt, with a lot of small water plants they were familiar with, growing around the rim of the pond. Farther down, the walls were rock. They showed lots of cool layers, like the walls of the ravine, but not nearly as smooth.

Alden could see the tip of their water pipe, too. They had lowered it a long way down, for just this type of reason, and it was a good thing, because the four-foot filtering point at the end of their pipeline was still completely submerged, but just barely.

The coolest thing to watch, and the thing most different from when the pond was full, was the surface of the water. It was so far recessed that the action of the spring was making the water churn a little. When the pond was full, it was calm. Alden allowed himself to relax a little and drift off in the soothing movement of the water surface, and before long, he drifted the rest of the way off and fell asleep.

The first thing Alden heard when he woke up, besides the constant humming of the nearby water pump, was some rustling from the forest. It sounded close. He sat up, and instinctively called out.

"Dad? Mom?"

The rustling intensified, but moved away. Some of the ground foliage was a little taller than Alden, and a lot of it wasn't, but from a sitting position, there was no hope of seeing anything.

Alden stood up, and noticed that his shirt rubbing on his neck was slightly uncomfortable. He'd gotten a bit of sunburn, but he was right about the forest shade, and it wasn't very bad. It would be gone tomorrow.

He moved around the edge of the pond to the creek bed on the far side, where the pond drained out through the deep forest. There was no more running water in it right now. Alden took a quick look back into the pond and noticed the water level was about halfway back up. The stream would be flowing again by the end of the day, which made Alden happy that it didn't seem like they'd ruined anything.

The cleared forest path continued next to the stream, but wasn't as well-maintained as the one next to the water pipe, as far as the pond. It was Alden's only hope for getting a look at whoever made that sound. He hurried down the path a ways, stepping over and around some low plants, then stopped.

"Hello?" he said. He paused, but there was no answer, and no rustling.

He could still hear the water pump, and he wanted to get all the way out of earshot so there was nothing to confuse what he heard. He kept going by the stream, wishing he could veer directly into the foliage, because he had a feeling he wasn't moving the same direction as the rustle-maker, but it was too thick to make any headway quickly. He stopped again, and everything was quiet.

"HELLO!"

Everything was still quiet.

This was really weird. There were no animals on the plateau. None that couldn't fly, anyway. Whatever this was had clearly moved through the ground foliage.

Then Alden had a terrible thought. It was the Grass Camp crew, or the supply ship crew, or somebody rescuing him, and he wasn't at the house. They were searching for him, and they could miss him.

He sprinted back past the pond and the water pump and down the path. He couldn't run the whole way without stopping for breath, but he only paused as long as he absolutely had to. He ran and ran, covering the trip in record time.

When he got to the edge of the forest, where the garden and irrigation tube were, he could see across all the open rock.

No ships. No buggies. No people.

He collapsed onto his hands and knees, heaving deep breaths, then looked up again to confirm. Nothing there.

Too tired to sprint anymore, he got up and walked as quickly as he could muster. He wouldn't be completely, totally sure until he was closer to the house. As he walked along the water pipe, though, everything stayed the same. No one appeared out of the rubble.

Had he missed them? They were in the deep forest brush when Alden started running. They couldn't have gotten back here faster than he did. They couldn't.

When he reached his safe distance from the building, he flopped down onto the ground and laid on his back to continue catching his breath and thinking about what happened. The thought that he'd missed a search party was nagging him a little, but he convinced himself that a person looking for him would have followed the path, just like he did. They would know that's where he'd be. So if it wasn't a person, what was it?

Alden really wanted to go back into the forest and search for whatever had made that noise. That was a long way off, though, and could be a lot longer, especially if it was some kind of animal that could get on and off the plateau, and wasn't even there to be found anymore. Besides, he needed food and water badly. What with his nap and all, the sun was well past midday. Thinking of the sun reminded him he also needed something for his head and neck. Out here in the open, his burn would get worse pretty fast now.

Alden stood and looked around. It was the first time he really paid much attention to all the stuff that was blasted away from the house by the explosion. A lot of it was just splintered bits of wood and random chunks of the composite walls, but there were household items, too. Some of them might still be OK.

The first thing to fix, though, was food. He was a little scared about that, because he really didn't have any idea what to do to get food. Beyond things like an occasional sandwich, he didn't fix food. Mom was the meal planner, and eating was fairly regimented. He got lots of food he liked; that was never an issue. He just didn't get snacks for himself much. Unapproved food outside of the schedule was frowned upon, mostly because of monthly resource preparations. Mom seemed to have an entire month of meals in her head at all times, and she was not fond of surprises when it came time to request the right things from the supply ship.

This time, he had it fairly easy. He didn't remember a lot from being in the refrigerator, but he knew there were things besides globs of cherry pie and some water bottles. Whatever was in there wouldn't last forever, and he should see what it is. There was the chest freezer, too. They didn't use the freezer portion of the refrigerator much, but the chest was packed with stuff. He couldn't remember seeing it, though.

The refrigerator was on the far side of the house, and Alden walked in his safe circle around to the back where the appliances were. Now that he was paying more attention to everything on the ground, he kept an eye out for something to wear on his head. He was on the side of the house where the lab was, and there were some bent shelves and shards of specimen bottles and smashed equipment. Farther away, something caught his eye, and he ran out to it with some excitement. It was perfect—the safari hat his dad wore. It was tan, hard plastic with a wide brim and webbing inside for his head. A small piece had been chipped out of the top of it, no doubt from banging around on the rock, but the hole wasn't much bigger than Alden could put his finger through, and didn't matter at all. He wouldn't have been ready to admit it yet, but part of his excitement was knowing he already had something of his father's to remember him by. It was large for his head, but he found an adjustment to tighten the webbing some, and made it work.

With Dad's safari hat giving his face and neck some needed shade, he continued toward the back of the house, also making better mental notes about what was around there. About twenty feet away from the refrigerator was the stove, looking fairly mangled. One side was crushed in, the burner surface was somewhere else entirely, and several metal panels were pulled away and twisted up. Given the condition of the stove, Alden was surprised the refrigerator hadn't popped open, but he thought of how difficult it was to break the melted seal, and figured that's what kept it closed.

Another forty feet farther from the house was the generator. Before the explosion, it had been installed outdoors, a few feet outside the back wall. It had some pipes and gauges and whatnot that weren't there anymore, but it was basically round, so it just rolled away, which was why it went farther than the other appliances.

Alden looked around for the chest freezer, but it didn't seem to be in that same area. Then he noticed something much closer to the house. He didn't want to believe it was the freezer, but he knew it was. It was all black, resting on its side with the top open. He couldn't tell if anything that used to be in it was lying around, because everything on the ground was dark over there. It was all way too far inside his safe circle for him to think about checking it out, and if it had all been in the fire and lying out in the sun since then, it was worthless, anyway. Alden quickly convinced himself it wasn't really that big of a loss, since things from the freezer had to be cooked, and he couldn't do that. Moreover, he couldn't keep anything cold, so even if he saved it all, he would just watch most of it spoil.

Resigned to the loss of all the freezer food, Alden went to the refrigerator and creaked the door open. This time, he could do it without standing on top. Inside, it was more of a mess than he remembered. Most of the mess was from a jar of mayonnaise, which had been mostly full and was now virtually empty. That and the cherry pie flying around inside made for an interesting salad of contents. There hadn't been a lot of cold leftovers. There rarely were; Mom's meal planning was more efficient than that. He was looking for something nutritious and easy, and he was lucky enough to find it: half of a ham. Ham was perfect; it lasted a long time, and it was ready to eat.

In this case, it was also slimy with mayo and pie guts, and Alden didn't exactly have any towels handy. He thought about using his shirt, but he didn't want to have to run to the irrigation tube to wash off every time a mess came up. The ham was about the size of a tiny watermelon chopped in two. Alden touched it to see if it was still cold at all. It wasn't. He picked it up, and immediately it slid out of his hands and onto the ground, flat side down.

The ground was rock, though, and out here away from the forest it didn't have a lot of loose dirt on it. Some. Alden picked up the ham again and looked at it. There was some dust and sand, but still pretty much just in the slime layer. He swiped across it with his hand, and it looked great. He wiped the rest of it the same way, flicking cherry mayonnaise off his fingers as he went, then lifted it to his mouth and took a bite out of the corner.

This was the best thing Alden had ever put in his mouth.

When he was done, he'd polished off roughly half of it, and he thought about what to do with the rest. Not that he had a lot of options. He couldn't make things cold anymore. He had no containers, and no way to keep dust off of anything except inside that refrigerator. He set the ham back in it, took out a bottle of water—which was also warm now—and closed the door. As much as he wished he could save it, he knew the ham had to be what he ate until it was gone, or it would go rotten.

He wiped some slime off the water bottle with his hand, twisted it open, and drank half of it. He capped it and looked around absent-mindedly as if to think of a place to put it, but that was pointless. He had another two bottles in his cave, and the refrigerator was still as good a place as any, so he cracked the door open, put his half-bottle inside, and let it close. Just to make sure about the freezer compartment, he climbed up on the refrigerator and tugged at the freezer door until it gave way. It was empty—they'd kept nothing but ice in there, and it was long gone.

That was a lot of ham Alden just ate, and in a hurry. His tummy wasn't feeling the best, and since he had no real plans for what to do next, he ambled off for his cave, to sit down and get out of the sun for a little while.

Being in his cave felt good. The last time he was there, he was a bit disturbed by how it did not feel the same, but this time it was comforting. It was a place that by contrast was not different from the day before, unlike everything outside. Resting felt good, too, after all that running in the sun and stuffing down lots of ham. He started thinking about what to do next, and reaffirmed his earlier plan that it needed to be looking around for stuff on the ground he could salvage. Between the refrigerator and the cave was the side of the house where the bedroom was, and he could see scattered clothes that might have survived. He'd need those.

Alden was suddenly tired. Tired from food and running, and already tired of having to think about how to deal with this. Getting over that would be essential in the time to come. He swiveled a little and laid back on his log, and in short order he was fast asleep.

Chapter 5

When I think back over that time, it is all crystal clear in my mind. All of it. At the same time, it feels like a completely separate, distinct life. It's mine, but not mine, as if I watched it happen. In fact, I feel like there were three unique lives: one before the murders, one after them on Cappa Terse, and the one I live now. But they're not all my life. It's like each time was a reincarnation. The transitions were so abrupt, and the circumstances so wildly different, that my mind has disassociated with those other lives. I don't know why; frankly, they were amazing experiences and I would love to feel like I own them. One thing, at least: my consciousness hasn't blanked them out. It may not acknowledge them, but it certainly remembers them. In vivid detail.

There were a number of pivotal moments through

that young Alden's life after the murders, but the one that set the course of it more than any other occurred on just the second day.

Alden hadn't counted on just how tired he really was. Most of it was probably from the emotional draining, but for whatever reason, he slept on through until morning. The two logs in his cave were chunks cut from one they'd found in the forest that had been flattened quite a bit from the weight of another tree, just after they both fell together. It was easy to sleep on them, and he'd convinced his parents to let him spend the night out there before—one of the nights they needed the bedroom for themselves.

This time, he hadn't planned on it at all, but he stayed sound asleep until after the sun was up the next morning. He was jostled awake by finally rolling off the log.

He immediately heard a sound that was both startling and incredibly exciting. It was the hum of the supply ship! Alden had no idea they would come so soon—he was planning on at least another three weeks without them. He quickly came to a sobering realization, though: if they came now, it had to be because they were expecting check-in communications from someone, and neither he nor the Grass Camp could send a signal.

Even as this thought was passing through his mind, he heard the sound changing. The ship was moving. He had to get topside immediately.

Alden scrambled to his feet and lunged at the ladder, skipping the bottom rung. His leap came down too heavy on the second one, and it snapped. His grip wasn't prepared for that, and he tumbled back onto the floor of the cave.

The sound was fast fading away.

He got back up again, and with slightly more measured actions, quickly climbed the ladder to the surface. The supply ship was already in the distance, off to the south, the direction they took on their way back to ECOP. It was well past the rocky edge of the ravine and moving away.

Alden screamed and waved his arms. "I'm here!"

He started running after them. "*I'm here!*"

Panic-stricken, he sprinted past the house, past the appliances, and out into the open rock terrain, yelling and waving. Most of that was after he couldn't even see them anymore.

He slowed up and stopped, then fell to his knees in utter disbelief. He missed them. The supply ship came and went, and he missed them. He put his face in his hands. How could this happen? How could this be happening to him? Why? It was difficult to even process what this meant.

Alden could feel the enormous wave of emotions about to burst forth, when his attention was oddly distracted by a pair of his mother's hiking shorts catching on his heel as it blew across the ground in the wind. He hadn't even realized it yet, but it was a very blustery day. Still sunny, like most days, but quite breezy.

He looked around across the open rock and saw a number of things being slowly but surely pushed around. Small books and clothes, mostly, and some rolling cans.

In an instant, he realized exactly what his situation meant. If no one was alive on Cappa Terse but him, and the supply ship didn't know he was there, they might never be back. If they never came back, it was more urgent than ever that he would need every single thing he could find. Especially some of the single things that were making their way across the ground to the edge of the ravine.

It was a long way south of the house to the ravine.

Half a mile or more. Anything that fell would be in the deep brush, a very long way from the ladder at the bridge, which was far behind him. He'd never be able to retrieve it. He got up and ran, looking around at the stuff he was passing as he tried to get to the ravine and intercept whatever was about to go over. The farther he went, the thinner the field of items, which was good. Maybe he hadn't lost much yet.

Panting, he got near the ravine, just in time to see a can of something roll over the edge ahead of him. Cans had apparently been moving the fastest, because that was about all there was this far away from the house, and there weren't a lot of them. His brain kicked into game mode again, and he scanned the area for which can was ahead of the pack. He ran and picked one up, then scanned for the next one.

Alden had to cover a tremendous amount of territory to do this, and after only two cans, became very aware that running with cans in his hands was a lot harder. Plus, the only conceivable place to put anything out of the wind was his cave, and he couldn't possibly carry anything back that far without losing many other things. He thought a moment, then reached down with a can and set it on end. He looked at it a moment, and it didn't tip over, but he was wasting time. He was just going to have to trust that the wind wasn't strong enough to tip cans, just to roll them.

It was lots easier to run to the cans and stand them on end, and he did that with a dozen or so. As he worked his way back toward the house and began to see clothing blowing his way, he kept doing the same thing, catching the items that were the farthest along. It was easier to carry clothes, but he still couldn't afford to get his arms full. He also couldn't afford to be picky—some of the things were his, more were his folks' clothes, and some of them were more like rags, with parts burned or torn away. He grabbed them all, and each time he'd gathered a few, he found a can and stood the can on top of them, then kept going.

Closer to the house, there were some books flapping around, but they weren't moving very fast. Alden wanted those, but they would have to wait until all the available clothing and food was secured. Soon, he realized that in order to get this done he would have to go closer to the house than his safe distance. That made him feel a little queasy, but he kept his eyes where they needed to be—scanning for loose things—and charged ahead. He didn't go within the house foundation. The walls were pretty well demolished, but not right down to the rock. The foundation was outlined with a base row of concrete blocks. Besides, in his peripheral vision, it looked like everything inside was black. There probably wasn't anything he needed, and if so, it wasn't going to blow away over the concrete blocks.

He kept at it until he couldn't see anything moving. When he was satisfied that nothing important was escaping, he was overwhelmed with fatigue, and he shuffled out to his safe distance and collapsed on the ground.

Heaving with exhaustion in the windy sun, his thoughts again turned to focusing on why he had to do what he just did. He was going to need every scrap of anything he could find for the time ahead. Not that three weeks wouldn't have been really difficult if those things had blown away, but three weeks was nothing compared to ... he didn't know what. Alden was too scared to contemplate what he knew deep inside had just happened.

It wasn't even emotional for him. The impulse to cry was coming over him earlier, before the retrieval emergency, but now it had left. Instead of despair, it was a deep fear that filled him. Fear that the supply ship was gone for good, that he had whatever food was in those cans—if he could get into them—and then he would die there, alone. It was a fear so intense that it simply left Alden stunned.

The fear soon became defeat. Instead of wondering if the ship would ever be back, and what his situation would be if it didn't, he presumed it never would. It was silly to think there was a reason for it to return. For several minutes, he lay in the sun, wondering why he had gone through all the effort. What did it matter if he saved any food? He'd be dead soon enough either way. Let it blow away. In fact, maybe it was better to speed it up. He thought about rounding up the cans and throwing them in the ravine himself. Just get it over with. And who would care? If the ship left, it had to be because they thought he was dead. If everyone thought he was dead, what's the difference if he was?

The idea that everyone he ever knew was either dead or thought he was dead drifted around in Alden's mind for a little while. It was very strange. In his short life, Alden had been on Earth, in a space station, and two other planets, and had met a lot of people at ECOP and everywhere else along the way. All of those people were going to be moving on without any thoughts of him anymore. Not a single person in the universe would think of him, or look for him, or wonder about him. Not ever.

As this concept sank in a little, Alden felt something very strange. His tumultuous emotions left him. There was no fear, no despair, no defeat. His young mind was wiped clean. There was nothing but him and the universe, him and that planet, him and a slab of rock on the plateau. There would be plenty more emotional issues to come, but in that moment, there was an odd calm, a purging. It was not peace; it was full retreat. Not denial, either—he knew full well what his circumstances were. It was a calm born from overwhelming trauma, like the eye of a hurricane, but it was there nevertheless. It wasn't a happy, soothing calm, either; it was emotionless. He was simply a vacant being.

As if from some power outside himself, Alden sat up abruptly. He was suddenly bored. It was time to do something, to move around a little again. Not for any big reason, just because he'd feel better if he was walking. He stood.

Some ham sounded good. He was not far from the refrigerator, and he was curious if the ham was still OK. He ambled over to it, lifted the door, removed his partial bottle of water, and set it on the ground. Then he pulled out the ham and closed the door. He smelled it. It seemed OK. He wasn't exactly sure what it would smell like if he shouldn't eat it, but so far it still just smelled like ham. He leaned back on the refrigerator and munched some. It still tasted good, too. While he was chewing, he closed his eyes and let the stiff breeze blow past him, feeling the sensations of the sun, the wind, and the flavor of the ham in his mouth. He ate about half of what was there and put the rest back. It was one more meal, if it lasted that long. He picked up his water, leaned on the appliance again, and drank.

When he was finished, he realized he had nowhere to throw his bottle away. They saved waste materials to be taken away by the supply ship every month, but now, no wastebasket, no airtight waste bins, no ship. Maybe something would come to him later, but for now he tossed it back in the refrigerator.

Most of the day was still ahead of him. Alden felt purposeless, but the only thing of interest to him at all was still rounding up salvageable items. His choices were essentially to pick stuff up or sit around and meditate, and he wasn't much for that. He chose picking up stuff. The only place to put anything was in his cave, so he walked over to one of his little piles of clothes with a can sitting on it, grabbed them, and headed off to his cave. He stopped along the way at another little pile and took those things, too.

The cans were both kidney beans. He enjoyed those.

When he got to his cave, he almost just dropped his things inside, but realized the fall might rupture the cans. It was a good ten feet to the bottom of the cave, and being shoved and blown around by the explosion and the wind was different from falling ten feet to a rock surface. It would be silly to have gone through so much to save the cans already, then ruin them at the point he finally had them safe.

He climbed down in one-handed and set the things down on a log. There were two logs in his cave, along two opposite walls, with eight feet of cave floor between them. The ladder came down to the floor portion. He picked one log to be the one to pile stuff on, and was thinking the other would have to be his shelter. Sitting, sleeping—everything was going to pretty much be on that log.

His father's safari hat was still down there, and he took it, put it on, and climbed back out for another trip. Just like when he was dashing madly to save stuff, it seemed to Alden he'd feel better if the trips got shorter and shorter instead of the other way around, so he walked out to where the farthest things were, to work his way closer. Without having to run, he could carry several more cans, so he collected an armload and headed back to the cave. He had too much to carry down the ladder, so he put things on the ground at the top of the ladder, then went up and down a few times to grab them and move them onto what was now his supply log.

Out and back, out and back, stopping every now and then at the refrigerator for a gulp of water. As he revisited all his tiny stockpiles, he was pretty happy to see that everything had stayed where he put them with the cans on end—"happy" being a relative thing within the blank countenance that overrode his attitude.

It took quite a while to retrieve everything, and he moved at only a moderate pace, but he didn't really stop to rest for any substantial period until all the cans, clothes, and a few books were safely in his cave. All accounted for, he had thirty-seven cans of things he could eat, dented and beat-up to various levels but intact. He had meat, with tuna, salmon, and chicken; vegetables, largely made up of several types of beans with some corn thrown in; and fruit. Mostly peaches.

In clothes, he had a variety of things across the board; he had an assortment of socks, underwear, pants, and shirts of his own, of Dad's, and of Mom's. He had one shoe that had belonged to each of his parents; not the best situation, but at least they were left and right. He also found the only dress his mom had at the camp, a yellow sundress. The top was burned away. All he had was from the waist down.

It was late afternoon, and the sun was about to be gone. Even though Alden thought it might be best to get used to being hungry, and he figured he could go the rest of the day without anything, he was also concerned that the ham wouldn't last much longer, and it would be a shame to waste it. He climbed out of the cave and made one last trip for the day, to the refrigerator.

The ham had no real smell to it much at all, which surprised him, but neither did he smell anything bad. He took a bite, and it tasted OK still. He decided to risk it, since food was at a premium. He was less careful about using up the bottled water, knowing the available water from the spring pond was all right. He gurgled down half a bottle and went back to his cave.

Alden's mind was still unwilling to think deeply about his situation or how he felt about it. There wasn't, and would never be, any way to have evening light other than his cave lantern, and something told him the fuel in that was another precious commodity he shouldn't use up frivolously. Rather than stare blankly into the darkness of the cave walls, he took a couple of shirts for covers and settled in for sleep, wondering if he would ever spend any night any differently than this.

Chapter 6

Alden awoke with the early sun, the rays beginning to splash on the cave wall near the top of his ladder. There wasn't really anything to do but go out and wander around looking for things from the wreckage he could still use, but he was getting tired and uncomfortable with the clothes he was wearing. He had more now, and he thought he might feel a little better if he got washed and changed, so that was his first project for the day.

Getting washed was itself something Alden needed to make a plan for, so he figured he might as well put a little thought into it. The only two places for running water were the stream in the forest and the stream in the ravine at the bridge. He couldn't really think ahead enough to predict all the things he might want or need running water for, but he knew water was going to be important. He remembered Dad describing how the water from the spring pond stream and waterfall fed the ravine stream, and it flowed under the bridge after it fell from the waterfall and made its way half-way around the plateau.

Alden was bright enough to put together that he didn't want to do anything in the forest stream that he didn't want to show up later in the ravine stream. He had already peed several places around the area—over the edge of the ravine, and into the water that was pumping out the back of the house before he shut off the main valve—but he needed a plan now. He'd been trained about collecting all those kinds of things in places where humans were not an indigenous animal; it's why their bathroom was elevated and everything drained into sealed containers. The supply ship carted those off and replaced them every month. He felt a little bit badly that he now had to pollute the planet, but at this point it was every man for himself, and he was the only man.

So, Alden's plan was to use the ravine stream point for washing himself and his clothes, and anyplace along the edge of the ravine downstream of the bridge for necessary business. He really had no choice but to trust that it was a natural process, and the rainy season would make everything right. Paper was still biodegradable, and natural business was one of the reasons Alden did want to save the books he found. It was the best he could do.

With this plan in mind, Alden picked out a set of clothes, put on his dad's safari hat, and hiked over to the bridge.

When he got there, the first thing he noticed as he glanced down into the ravine was that the buggy was not in the same position he'd left it in two days earlier, and the door was opened and pulled back. It was windy the day before, but Alden was pretty sure if the wind couldn't blow over a can of kidney beans it couldn't open a buggy door.

Alden screamed into the ravine.

"DAD!"

He dropped his clothes to the bottom and scurried down the ladder. Just as he had the fateful night of his birthday, he pulled and tugged and pushed his way through and over the brush to get to the buggy. This was too important to be scared, and when he reached it he immediately looked inside. Dad was gone.

Alden turned his head out into the ravine.

"DAD!"

He scrambled back through the brush to the cleared area. He stood, panting, and cupped his hands around his mouth.

"DAD! Dad I love you!"

The second bit surprised even Alden. He wasn't sure why that came out. It made him realize, though, that he knew this whole time Dad couldn't be out and about. Dad was gone. He knew that. He was just trying to tell him one more time before he said good-bye.

It was time for another crying session, the one where he began to come to terms with his loss. It was a long, exhausting sob, bellowing with the tragedy and unfairness of it.

When it was over, he was also coming to terms with what the supply ship had done. All while he was asleep in his cave, they came and searched and took the bodies. That meant Mom wasn't in the house, either.

But why didn't they find him? Why didn't they look harder? Why didn't they check his cave? Alden knew the supply ship crew had regular runs to camps on other planets. Cappa Terse was far from their only stop. After a few moments of contemplation, Alden realized if a ship was dispatched to their camp because of no communication, it probably wasn't a supply ship at all, really. And it wouldn't have been their regular crew. It would have been a rescue ship with a crew that had no idea about Alden's cave.

The house foundation was almost entirely black. Even if Alden had been thinking Mom was in the house, maybe she kind of wasn't. Maybe she'd been burned up completely. If she was, they'd think Alden had been, too. They probably took some ashes with them thinking they were Alden's remains when they were probably just his pillow.

Yes. This was exactly what he thought it was. He was here alone. Alive and alone, and always would be.

Not that this realization meant he was dealing with it in any comprehensive way, yet. That would have been too overwhelming. He was still holding back on most of this awareness, letting little bits into his thoughts, like a water valve. Not like the irrigation hose that knocked him over; more like the faucet he could only turn on for a few seconds when he needed it, because they didn't want to overflow the sealed containers.

This was now about eleven-year-old Alden finding a way to survive on his own, for the rest of his life, with thirty-seven cans of food.

Time to get himself washed up and change his clothes.

Alden took everything off and stepped into the stream. He'd been in it before. It was cool, but not cold, which he was thankful for, since he had no way of heating water. It was a dozen feet wide and up to his knees in the deep spots. The current was steady but not strong enough to push him downstream very hard. There was dirt along the banks of the stream, but in the creek bed itself there were mostly large, flat rocks. Like the spring pond, the water was magnificently clear and clean, and Alden chose a rock and sat down, facing upstream so the water came at him.

The coolness flowed around him in a wonderfully refreshing cascade. He hadn't experienced it like this, and it was newly invigorating, surprisingly so under the circumstances. He liked that he found it easy to let his thoughts wander away from him and just enjoy the renewal of the babbling current. He bent forward and let some of the water run into his mouth, and drank. It was like taking in pure nature.

Alden sat like that for some time, not wanting to spoil it with things that needed to be done or dealt with.

Eventually, he stood and walked over to his clean clothes. He was just now recognizing that he hadn't found any shreds of any towels, and unless he used other clothing, would not be able to dry off after washing. No matter. Not for now, anyway. There was plenty of daytime sun ahead to dry him off. He got dressed, with socks and shoes last as he stepped back over to the edge of the stream to rinse the dirt off his feet before he put them on. He left the dirties there. He would need to wash them right there, and they weren't going anywhere in the meantime, even if it got windy. They were already at the bottom of the ravine.

He got himself mentally prepared for wandering through more rubble, including deciding he needed to look through the blackness of the house foundation. It was time. He put on his safari hat and climbed the ladder.

At the top, he met an amazing sight. Off to the north, at the edge of the forest, was an animal. A walking animal! It was hard to tell for sure, but it looked like one of the huge, rhinoceros-type things. His Grass Camp friends had called it a burlon. It was just standing there, nibbling on some foliage.

Disregarding any thought of danger, Alden took off running toward the thing. How could this be? There were no animals. None he'd ever seen, anyway. None like this, that's for sure. It had to be what was rustling in the forest the other day.

When he was still hundreds of feet away, the burlon saw him, and turned and lumbered into the forest. Alden instinctively yelled after it.

"No! Wait!"

By the time Alden reached the edge of the forest, the burlon was out of sight. It was deep and far away; Alden couldn't even hear it rustling.

"Come back!"

That was wishful thinking, but fruitless. Alden knew there was no way for him to effectively track or follow the beast in the deep forest. He'd have to wait until the animal came out to the edge again.

Alden turned and began walking back toward the house, thinking about what he'd just seen. That was really impressive. It was amazing. Not just an animal on the plateau, but one of those big burlons. Mom and Dad would have been beside themselves. So would the Grass Camp. Now, he couldn't show anyone. He couldn't even take a picture of it. He spent a few moments dealing with the reality that everything he experienced from then on was only for him, and then tried to focus again on the wonder of it.

There couldn't have been an anomaly like a burlon on the plateau without something strange happening. Maybe there was another way on or off the plateau. If a burlon could do it, so could Alden. This could be big. If he could get off the plateau, he could get to the Grass Camp and see what happened there. Maybe the Grass Camp looked like his house did, but maybe not. Regardless, it was the only conceivable place on the planet where he might be able to find help or a way to help himself. He had to get to the Grass Camp.

Alden had a big project now. Not just staying alive

for no reason. He needed a way off the plateau, and the burlon meant there could be a way. He just had to find it. In order to find it, he had to be able to search the plateau. All of it. There were still large sections in the deeper areas that none of Alden's family had explored yet. To do that, he would need more tools, something besides his hands to help get him through the thick brush in the deep forest.

He decided his next step was still combing the wreckage for salvage, but now it was different. Now it wasn't just the only logical thing to do, it was something with a purpose. Purpose was good. More. Purpose was critical. Purpose could keep him alive.

When Alden got back near the house, he decided the first step was to face his fears about going inside the foundation and looking around. The most debris was closest to the house, so that's where his search needed to start, and he had to satisfy his thoughts about how and why Dad wasn't in the buggy anymore.

He paused before he got real close. This still gave him a touch of nausea, but he took a deep breath, let it out, and headed in. He decided it was going to be best if he charged right to the center of it, like ripping off a bandage quickly.

Everything was charred and black, and even after a day of hefty winds, it smelled strongly of burnt things. Wood, mostly, but some more irritating, like plastic or chemicals. There weren't many discernible objects inside the foundation. The burning had been intense. Everywhere he looked, he was scared, but he tried his best to fight through it and take a quick scan of where all the rooms had been, to get past the whole idea of finding Mom. There really wasn't anything to speak of. All the furniture in the living room and kitchen was cinder. All the interior walls were burned right down to nothing. He even found himself walking on ash-covered rock through parts of the house because the floor had burned away.

There was no longer any indication that the bathroom had been built up, although the base floor underneath it, where the containers were, was slightly less damaged than other places. He could make out a couple crumpled, melted containers, too. The container they were draining into must have emptied its contents and put out some of the fire in that area. That was pretty disgusting, but it had been early in the supply ship cycle, so there couldn't have been very much in it. Just the same, Alden decided not to walk right through there.

Along the back, where the appliances had been, he saw some black, mangled pieces of metal that he knew were from the fuel drums just outside the back wall, near the generator. This was why everything burned so much, and so hot. Their two drums exploded, and the house was immediately doused in fuel. Anything that didn't get blasted away into the surrounding area sat and burned in a fuel fire. Not much could survive that.

No people, either.

He realized that his fears about what the rescue ship crew had found were exactly true. There was no extended search for Alden because he and Mom were both presumed to be incinerated in this fire. Maybe they found some small remains of Mom and decided they were both in there. At any rate, there was nothing left. Nothing to see that would forever connect his memory of his mother to some little pile of ashes. He needn't be afraid of that, or of the house, any longer.

It was easy to conclude that everything inside the foundation of the house was worthless, so he stepped out the front door opening and started a clockwise search. He decided he would work away from the house in bigger and bigger circles, trying to cover everything and make sure he knew where he'd been.

His first trip around didn't turn up much, but that was no surprise. Everything had gotten really hot, and the fuel had sprayed a lot of area outside the house foundation, too. Especially in back, the open rock was darkened by having a coating of fuel burn away there.

A little farther away from the house, though, he began finding things he could use. As he made a couple of circles, he was noticing some patterns in how things got blown out and where the worst damage was. The east side, facing the bridge, was the living room side; it was also closest to the fuel drums. There was almost nothing of value there, both because the living room had nothing helpful to begin with, and because the fuel fire was most intense there.

The north side, where the front door opened to face the forest, was where the lab and bathroom were, and also didn't have a lot of salvageable stuff. The east side, though, was the bedroom side, and that's where most of the clothes had been. That side was closest to Alden's cave.

The south side, looking out over the majority of the open rock, was the real gold mine: the kitchen and storage room were both there. Besides the appliances, all the food cans had basically been thrown to the south, as were other small kitchen things. Not the ultramicrowave or other small appliances—they were there, but they were destroyed—but small hand tools. All the metal stuff. Silverware, a couple of larger utensils, and the happiest find of all for the moment: a hand-crank can opener. Alden actually yelled into the air and danced around when he found it.

There were other metal hand tools from the storage room, too. Things that really had more to do with saving Alden's life than anything else he found that day. He had a hammer, a hatchet, and a machete. He'd seen their chain saw, but that was badly bent, so the sharp tools were critical. He set aside other things as well, like the screwdriver blade he found. The handle had been crushed or melted off. He'd found a garden hoe with the long handle snapped in two about half-way up. He didn't see a pair of pliers and thought that might come in handy, but there was a lot of building debris. When he had more time to pick up or turn over every charred fragment of wall or roof, he might discover more, but considering the way the landscape looked at a glance, he was very pleased with his treasures.

He also came across something he knew he would have to take great care not to lose in the ravine or allow to blow away. Alden found a large cooking pot with a curved handle across the top that flopped to the side when not in use. The pot was dented up, but not with any holes. It was covered in soot, but that could be wiped away. Of everything he had looked at or collected since the explosion, that pot was his only container. Water, food, tools—anything and everything he would ever need to carry from one place to another would be carried in that pot.

Everything Alden found was carted off to his cave and piled up on his log. With another day of salvage operations behind him, he lay down and pulled his cover shirts up over him. He didn't realize it, but his new life was only three days old and his mind was already adjusting in curious ways. It wouldn't be possible to remain emotionally devastated, or even vacant, for very long. He was beginning to adapt, and as he drifted off to sleep, Alden thought about how much fun it would be to attack the deep forest with his machete in the morning.

Chapter 7

Alden was up with the sun, and when he climbed out of his cave with his safari hat, a bottle of water, and his machete, a bolt of excitement hit him. At the edge of the forest was the burlon again. Alden's nerves were prickling as he started off toward it, walking quietly this time. It was quite a ways off, but Alden was fascinated to watch it move. Mostly it just raised and lowered its head, and Alden figured it was eating something.

He had no idea what he would do if he actually got near the animal. It could be really dangerous. He knew it ate plants, but maybe it ate boys, too. It was a risk he was willing to take. This was far too exciting not to see whatever he could see.

As Alden got closer, he slowed some more, and when he was only a hundred feet away, the animal looked up right at him. Alden froze, partly from nervous fear and partly to try not to scare the burlon away.

They looked at each other for the better part of a full minute. Alden was marveling at this beast. Here it was, an actual wild animal, standing right in front of him. It was a tremendous animal, too. Taller than Alden at the shoulders, with thick-looking, dark grey and brown mottled skin. It was big around, with its back arching up a little and a saggy belly underneath, between short, stout legs. Its head protruded forward with a slightly jutting forehead and a rounded snout. The most impressive feature, though, was a bony plate all the way around its neck, just behind the head. The plate angled back toward its body and came to a series of short, dull points all around, giving the burlon a decidedly prehistoric flair.

Alden stared in amazement, and the burlon stared back.

The two of them were situated at the outer edges of the vegetable garden—Alden just outside the outer edge, and the burlon standing in the first row nearest the forest. Alden decided to take another step forward. The burlon stayed motionless. Alden took two more steps, and the animal still didn't move. Alden began walking very slowly, locked with the animal's gaze and ignoring the plants beneath his feet, but on his third step he stumbled in an irrigation rut, and the burlon turned and lumbered away into the forest.

"Wait!" said Alden as he righted himself and started to run, but it was obvious the burlon could gallop considerably faster than Alden could chase. By the time Alden even got to where the burlon had been standing, the beast far outdistanced him. It was pointless to pursue, and Alden pulled up and stopped in disappointment.

He heaved a sigh and looked around where the burlon

had been. He was right about the eating. A whole bunch of carrot plants were gone. Alden knew the garden fairly well, because the gardening was something he and his parents did a lot of together. It was some of Alden's basic education, and he was a good student, especially with things his mom and dad showed and explained directly. He was less fond of book learning; more of a hands-on type of guy. He hadn't actually given the garden much thought yet, despite the obvious nature of it being his only renewable food source, because he was somewhat intimidated by it. He knew some things about the plants, but he wasn't a key player in the overall garden planning, and now he was going to have to figure out how to manage this himself.

One good thing about the garden was that the climate on the plateau was pretty warm year-round. Cooler in the rainy season, but never approaching frost or snow. That meant they could stagger their crops so they were constantly about to harvest something. The bad part about that was the constant rotation took strategy, and Alden was going to be faced with a lot of trial-and-error gardening that could cost him lots of food. Also, the warm weather kept the cool-weather crops at a little less than their best, but they tried them, anyway, just for the variety.

Alden did know that the carrots—one of the cool-weather crops—were almost to harvesting; he also knew that, in spite of the plentiful availability of seeds from ECOP, Mom and Dad were trying to see if they could bring some carrot plants to seed there on the plateau. That required a second year of growing for those plants, and a burlon eating up the seed plants would not be helpful, or else this would be the last carrot crop. Those were at the other end of the row, though, and hadn't been disturbed yet.

As he glanced over the area of missing plants, Alden

thought he noticed something peculiar. He got down on a knee and looked a little closer. Along the row the burlon had been eating, there was a string of carrots with the greens eaten off, then a bunch of holes where they had been pulled up. It was a cinch that no burlon had ever had carrots before, but it looked like the animal had learned that the real treat was below the soil, and how to pull them out. This was a fascinating little discovery, and it gave Alden an idea for something to try during their next encounter.

That would not likely be soon, however, and Alden had a plan for the day. He would begin the hunt for some way that the burlon had made it onto the plateau. This meant traveling the edge of the ravine, all the way around, through lots of unexplored territory. He knew up front it would be many days of work. It took most of a day just to walk to the stream waterfall and back to the house, and that was more or less straight through the heart of the forest. The ravine edge went far around, and deep in the forest, the brush was thick right up to the ravine in many places. He would have to chop it away with his machete. Truth be told, it sounded like fun. Alden had a purpose, and some hope that this project would lead him somewhere that would somehow help him get off the planet and back to ECOP.

After that would be anyone's guess. He did have other family, and he assumed he'd stay with some of them, but thinking about that didn't seem real yet. It was too early. First things first. As Dad had taught him, just figure out the next step and take it. With a water bottle in his left hand and the machete in his right, he started off across the face of the front edge of the forest, to make his way out to the ravine and begin the trailblazing.

He knew the brush was dense along the ravine in spots because one of their really cool pieces of equipment was a drone aircraft with a camera, and they had done a bunch of remote surveys of the plateau and ravine. What those surveys had appeared to show was that the ravine walls were nearly vertical all the way around the plateau. The far walls on the other side of the ravine, too. In fact, the ravine wasn't just a single loop around the plateau. If it were, it would have just filled up with the water from the spring pond. The ravine loop creating the plateau was part of a much larger system of ravines, splitting and joining like veins across the landscape. Some of them were deeper than here, some shallower, or more narrow. But this seemed to be the only place where they formed a loop, creating the plateau island.

The ravine system extended off to the east and south of the ravine. To the west was the grassland, and that was continuous, all the way to the far bush territory and past that to some mountains. To the west was where most of the animals on Cappa Terse lived. The west was where the burlon came from. Somehow, the burlon came, so somehow, the drone camera surveys missed something. That something was what Alden was expecting to find.

He got to the edge of the ravine, looked down over it, set his machete on the ground, and took a sip of water. It tasted wonderful, and he wanted more, but he was trying to conserve it. He didn't want to be forced back to his cave earlier than he hoped by being too thirsty. His pockets weren't bulky enough for things like cans or bottles, and he didn't have enough hands to bring food, too, or else he'd have done that.

The ravine was beautiful. It was one of the reasons he used to enjoy going out on the bridge when he could sneak that in. On the plateau, the top surface rock was light brown in the open area, but in the walls of the ravine—and the spring pond, when he saw deep into it—had layers of different colors. They were all at a sloping angle, higher at the south end of the plateau where the house was, sloping lower where the forest was. At the forest, the surface was darker, a medium brown dirt, and Alden could see the darker layer in the walls of the ravine.

Farther down, toward the bottom of the ravine, were layers even darker, and redder, a maroon color. It was beautiful and intriguing, and always had Alden wondering about eons before and how the rock formed. Some of his studies covered the basics of geological striations—not the stuff every kid his age had covered, but he was on a program geared toward Pri Crew science. He loved learning about those things, then going outside and looking at it for himself, pondering the swirling, hot minerals that eventually cooled into what he was standing on. He was looking forward to seeing a lot more of the ravine with his own eyes instead of through the drone camera.

He took a deep breath through his nose. Even though the day was still, there was some of the aroma of the brushtops in the air, and a little of the scent of the thick bushes that filled the bottom of the ravine. In another month or so, they would have a different scent, one from their flowers, that would be much stronger. Not unpleasant, but slightly pungent. They bloomed a light blue, in flowers that closely resembled blue vinca, and the bushes were thick with them. In June or Arido, the ravine positively transformed for the two weeks the blooms were at their peak. Not only did the appearance change from the mass of green to a wall-to-wall river of light blue, but the whole river was alive with animals.

There were insects that used the nectar, and they came by the billions. There were birds that ate the insects, and they came by the thousands. The insects weren't bees, and couldn't sting, but they were so thick you certainly wouldn't want to climb down the bridge ladder into the ravine during blooming. Besides getting the bugs all over you, it could be really dangerous if you were attacked by confused birds. From above, though, there was the heavy scent of the flowers, the constant hum of insects, and the incessant cackling of the birds. All in all, an impressive scene.

The drone had showed them there were stretches where the bushes didn't grow down there, and Alden had considered whether to use the ravines to find his way somewhere useful, but the open places were few, and even if he made the effort to hack his way through the miles of dense brush, eventually he would be too far away from the plateau to ever use anything there, and he would be working his way farther and farther from the Grass Camp. There was no use for that plan.

Time to get to it. Alden picked up his machete and started along the rim. The first mile was pretty uneventful; there was an old, toppled log to climb over— one that had fallen with the brushtop hanging out into the ravine—but for the most part it was merely a hike along the ravine edge of the forest. Eventually, he reached where ground plants were getting bigger, and although it wasn't truly necessary yet, he was playfully swatting them out of his way with the machete. It was sharp, and he was making quick work of the thin shrubs.

After a time, perhaps two miles in, he was working quite a bit harder, and the growth was as tall as he was. It was also woodier, not just green and leafy. He paused and had some more water. This was what this project was always going to be about: hacking his way laboriously through all the dense brush around the north end of the plateau. Now that he was doing it, he found it was considerably more strenuous than his imagination had conjured.

He sat, and as he drank more water, the enormity of everything ahead of him loomed larger and larger in his mind. None of this should be happening. None of it should be necessary. Mom and Dad should be here. This is all wrong. No eleven-year-old kid should be out in the woods by himself trying to chop through the forest so he can find a way off a planet with a population of one.

He was tired of this already. He was hungry. Even if he went back to his cave, all there was to eat would be a cold can of vegetables. No hot hamburger or roast. No pie, no cookies, no sandwiches—nothing. Ever. It was insane.

Alden started to cry, and it quickly became a deep purging. His safari hat toppled to the ground as he sobbed hard in despair, but before long it turned to anger. He jumped up, took his water bottle, and in frustration hurled it into the ravine.

He picked up his machete in both hands and began flailing into the foliage, chopping and yelling.

Who would do this? Why? A house can explode, but the bridge? Somebody did all this on purpose. Somebody killed his parents and everybody at the Grass Camp on purpose. That's just crazy. Crazy. Why couldn't ECOP stop this? Who would want this to happen?

They have to pay.

In his mind, Alden was hacking at an unknown evil, a murderous villain who had taken everything from him.

It only lasted a few seconds, only until the peak of the rage was out. Alden collapsed onto his knees and dropped the machete. He put his hands on both sides of his head, slowly crumpled down until his head was on the ground in front of his knees, and cried some more.

Chapter 8

With heaving, sniffling breaths, Alden lay on the forest floor, spent. His rage and frustration were real, but now the reality of dealing with his situation set in again. He sat up and put his safari hat on. He was facing back toward the path he had cleared along the edge of the ravine, and although he was immediately struck with a positive thought that he had covered more ground than he would have guessed, something else was far more riveting.

Standing at the beginning of his path, a hundred feet away, was the burlon.

Alden wanted to get to his feet quickly, but without scaring the animal. He stood as smoothly as he could, and the burlon didn't move. Alden decided to speak to it.

"Have you been watching me?" he said. "I'll bet you're

wondering what I'm doin' out here, huh."

There was no reaction from the burlon.

Alden began taking steps toward it, but kept speaking, hoping that would keep the animal's attention or curiosity so he could get closer than last time.

"I'm just tryin' to find out how you got here, buddy," Alden said. He kept moving, and reached out a hand. "We've never seen anything like you on the plateau before. You're not dangerous, are you? All you eat is plants. You like carrots, don't you? Carrots are delicious."

Alden kept up like that, closer and closer. It was working. It seemed like his voice was helping, making him less of a threat. Then, when he was still about thirty feet off, the burlon suddenly bolted and charged away.

"Hey! No! It's all right!" said Alden. He dropped his hand and let out a sigh. It was a little disappointing, but also encouraging that he got so much closer this time. He was determined to make contact with the burlon. This wildlife encounter was easily the most fascinating thing ahead of him in his life on the plateau.

It was now a number of hours into his day, and Alden thought it was time to make the hike back to the cave for food and water. He went back for his machete, then set off on the trek. When he got to the garden, he paused at the carrot rows. He went along past the ones he knew were seed plants, then stopped and pulled a few of the eating crop. It wasn't terribly easy, and he wondered how the burlon had managed to figure it out, but for Alden, once he worked his machete into the dirt around them it was a cinch.

He liked raw carrots, and he knew he would need to make good use of the crop, so even though it was a little early for them, he decided to have a carrot lunch. The shallow soil and climate at the edge of the forest made for short, stumpy carrots that were a little tart and green at the top of the root, but it was better than no carrots.

If the burlon liked them, Alden was thinking he might be able to use them to help get closer. Having carrots to offer would make him much more appealing. He pulled ten—five for his lunch and five to save for the burlon—and continued on toward his cave.

When he got there, he was reconsidering his traveling equipment. It was a long way into the deep forest from the cave, and having to come back in the middle of the day was going to waste a lot of time. Also, pulling the carrots had made him think about harvesting in general, and his pot would help him carry vegetables, but he needed something else. Something hands-free would be best.

He looked through the clothing he had, to see if he could make something out of those, but he was really hesitant to use anything he could actually wear. Then he saw his mother's dress. He paused, because he kind of wanted to just preserve it as a memento, but he also knew he was going to have to use anything he could the best way he could. It's what she would have wanted.

Alden took the dress, which was missing the very top portion above the waist. He bunched the top end together and knotted it closed. Then he played around with how the other end could hang or be carried. In the end, he decided he had to make two rips in it from the bottom hem up into the dress, then tie the two bunches of fabric together at the hem. That made a loop he could put over one shoulder. He tried it on and smiled. This was going to work pretty well. He had a pouch now, one that could hold lots of stuff—tools, water, cans, harvested crops—and he could work with both hands if he needed to. It also made him feel good that he would have one item from each parent with him at all times: his safari hat from Dad, and sundress pouch from Mom. In that way, they would both be with him, helping him work all day.

His carrots were still dirty, and there was a lot to do, so Alden packed the carrots, a bottle of water, and the garden trowel in his pouch and headed off. He was still carrying the machete; that was a little big for the pouch, and it seemed a sure thing it would make big rips in the dress material.

Alden had considered just using bottled water to wash the carrots, which would have been fine since he could refill the bottles, but it seemed wasteful somehow. These bottles he had were still the original bottled water from the fridge, and it felt different. It just felt wrong to dump that water his family had in their house over some dirty carrots.

As he was deciding how else to wash them, though, another thought occurred to him. He could use the stream water in the ravine or the irrigation tube water, and the irrigation tube was on the way to the forest, so that was his choice. The realization he had, though, was that the water pump for the irrigation tube was still running constantly. Earlier, this was not a concern, because the supply ship was going to be there before it could have possibly mattered, but now things were different. He had no idea how long he was going to need the pump to be available, and with no way to do any maintenance or repairs, he was going to have to shut the pump down and save on wear and tear. It was best if he did that now.

When he got to the irrigation tube valve, he turned it on, but only part way. The stream of water was still far more than he needed to wash carrots in, and he held them one by one in the flow, rubbing each as he had seen his mother do. When he finished cleaning the last one, he took a bite of the delicious, crunchy freshness. With the rest of the clean carrots in his pouch, he shut off the valve and headed into the forest toward the spring pond path.

The forest was calm. The sweet scent of the brushtops mixed with the chirps of birds flitting between the trees. He nibbled some more on his carrot. For a moment, Alden felt like he used to, when walking into the forest was for nothing but searching and discovery. That life was gone forever, but in Alden's young mind he clung to that memory, knowing that if he let himself feel nothing but the pain, he might just as well jump in the ravine.

Not today. Marching across the carpet of dead brushtop vines, Alden decided not to die that day. It was a decision he remembered making as he stood at the base of the bridge that first terrible morning after his birthday, and would need to make again and again if he expected to live out his days anywhere other than Cappa Terse. Today was not as traumatic, but it was good to revisit his father's words about just taking the next step, and right now that was making his way to the pump by the spring pond.

For the next twenty minutes, Alden hiked the familiar route, finishing his carrot and another. Then, he heard a distant sound that was just like his footsteps in the dry vines, but didn't quite match his gait. He stopped and listened.

Rustle, rustle.

Emerging from the thicker foliage ahead, where the spring pond path began, came the burlon. It was walking toward him. Alden could tell the animal was getting more and more curious about him, just as he was about the burlon. He set his machete on the ground, reached into his pouch, and pulled out two carrots. Unless he'd been imagining it, talking seemed to ease the nervousness, so he spoke.

"Hey there, buddy," said Alden. The burlon was still far enough away that Alden wasn't entirely sure if he could be heard, but he didn't want to raise his voice and sound like he was yelling.

The burlon kept moving slowly forward, and Alden decided to do the same, with the carrots held out in front of him so the animal could plainly see the bait. Alden intentionally left the green tops on the carrots so he could do exactly this, and he held the carrots by the greens so they would dangle a little.

The two of them slowly closed half the gap between, then the burlon paused. Alden held up, also, both to match the burlon's behavior, and to not appear aggressive. This time, with his bait, he was going to try to get the beast to come to him instead of approaching it and scaring it off.

"I've got a treat for you," said Alden, waving the carrots gently.

To Alden's delight, the burlon began moving again.

"That's right, buddy, these are really tasty. I know you like 'em. These are fresh and clean and super delicious."

The burlon was still slowly walking.

"Come and get it, burly," Alden said. "Yeah, that's it. That's a good name. Burly. Come on, Burly."

When there was still fifteen feet to go, Burly stopped. Alden could sense that this was no time to act excited. Stay the course. Just be calm and soothing. His arm was tired and he switched hands with the carrots, but kept the prize out in front of him, chest-high, roughly the height of Burly's head. He kept talking.

"I'm your friend. Everything's all right. Come on over and get the carrots."

Burly started again. Alden's nerves tingled sharply, as he could now hear Burly's breaths huffing. His eyes were large and dark brown and not at all menacing, in contrast to his body. Alden knew if this animal chose this moment to freak out and charge, he could swat Alden right off the plateau with a single nudge.

This was magnificent.

Alden's own breathing got faster as Burly slowed but did not stop until his head was only two feet away from the carrots.

"Holy cannoli," Alden said softly. It was an expression from a character in a game he liked to play. He didn't actually know what cannoli was, but he liked the sound of it.

"I won't hurt you," said Alden. "I would never, ever hurt you."

As if understanding that final reassurance, Burly took a small step, reached and twisted his head, and snatched the carrots away.

Alden was speechless now. It worked! This enormous, spectacular beast was right in front of him, and he just fed it carrots. Alden could see the cavernous wrinkles in Burly's skin, and the thin, light hairs that grew around his mouth. He saw his teeth, blunt and yellow and bigger than Alden's thumbs. And he smelled him, musty and earthy.

Moving as smoothly as he could, Alden took the last two carrots from his pouch. He held them in front of him, but not at arm's length. Burly would have to come even closer for these two.

"Come on, boy," Alden said, thinking to himself how silly it would look to see an eleven-year-old talking to this majestic brute like a puppy. Completing the picture, Burly took two steps up to Alden and relieved him of the carrots. Alden satisfied his intense curiosity and reached out with his other hand to touch Burly's snout, laying it between his nostrils. Alden expected Burly to yank his head away at this move, but he didn't. Alden felt the coarse, grey skin moving rhythmically as Burly chewed his carrots.

"Those are good, huh," Alden said.

Burly's bony collar was outrageously unlike anything Alden had seen before. Just behind his head, it went all the way around his neck, larger on top and curving up as it guarded his shoulders. It was easily six feet across and at least an inch thick, and the dull points all around looked battle-worn, as if they were once wickedly sharp and now bore the marks of a life well-led.

"You've been around a while, haven't you, boy," said Alden.

The chewing stopped, and Burly lifted his snout a little. Alden took his hand away. "What is it?"

Burly pushed his head forward a little, toward Alden's side, and nudged his pouch.

Alden chuckled. "More carrots? Sorry, Burly, that's all I brought."

Burly nudged the pouch again. Alden put both hands inside it, then pulled them both out and showed Burly his empty palms. "See?"

With his head raised slightly again, Burly made a deep noise, like a low moan. It made Alden's entire body vibrate. Burly was clearly unhappy about the size of his snack. He wasn't acting agitated, though. Just a mild complaint.

"We could go back and get more, buddy," said Alden, "but I have a feeling you'd eat my whole crop right now. We'd better wait." He held up his empty hands again. "No more."

Burly turned slowly away. Alden watched in wonder as the animal's body pivoted sideways, and he got a better look. The arching back that was taller than he was, the paunch of a belly that looked slightly softer than everything else, and the immensely powerful legs with three-toed hooves. He had to be at least fifteen feet long. It was amazing that he was as fast as he was when he galloped. Burly had a thick tail just long enough to curl a little on the ground, and it swished behind him as he began walking back toward the thicker foliage.

"That's it?" said Alden. Burly paused and looked back

over his shoulder for a moment, then kept walking. Alden had a fantastic notion. "Oh, wait, you want me to follow you." Alden had no idea if that was really true, but he sure wanted it to be. "All right, wait up."

Alden picked up his machete and hurried a little to catch up to Burly, who continued at his steady pace. That pace was a little quick for Alden, but he ran up alongside Burly's right shoulder and tried to keep up. Burly seemed unfazed by the minor commotion, unlike their previous encounters when he would have bolted for the deep forest. Alden took this as a wonderful sign that Burly was at least indifferent to Alden's presence, and just maybe really did intend for him to come along.

This whole experience was so far beyond what Alden had expected that he could hardly contain himself, but he tried to rein in some of his excitement. Silly as it seemed, he actually didn't want Burly to think he was too weird, and ruin their friendship before it could even get started. At this point, he'd follow Burly right off the waterfall if that's where he went. This was way, way better than anything he was going to do with the stupid water pump.

Chapter 9

As boy and burlon made their way toward the dense forest, Alden noticed early on that Burly was headed for the path to the spring pond. Every other time he'd seen Burly head into the forest, he took a more random route directly into the foliage. Alden decided this was another sign that Burly was doing it intentionally, that he knew the path was easier for Alden. This animal had to be really intelligent, and really observant, watching Alden's movements in the forest and his work clearing a path along the ravine ridge. Alden would have expected a burlon to be more of a simple wild animal behaving on instinct, but just in their short time together Burly was showing himself to be considerably more.

Burly pretty much took up the whole path, and Alden pulled back to follow behind him. That didn't keep

Alden from chatting away. He'd had no one to talk to for days.

"That louder chirp is from the blue birds," Alden said as he would have to anything with ears. "They're mostly up in the tops of the trees. We call these brushtops, 'cause all the vines come down from the top. Guess we could have called 'em vinetops, but brushtops does sound a little bit better. The higher chirps are from those smaller brown birds with red heads. We just call those redheads. They come down into the forest more than the blue birds do, but we still don't know where they live. We haven't seen any nests yet. My mom and dad say that—"

Alden paused there, and rephrased. "Well, Mom and Dad used to ..."

He was suddenly overwhelmed, and he quit walking.

"Mom and Dad are ... "

Alden felt like he somehow needed to say it out loud, but he was already crying and couldn't make the words. He plopped down and sat in the path as Burly kept moving on. Alden put his face in his hands and wept. Speaking to Burly brought it up in a different way, and forced him to face it outside his silent thoughts, even if this poor animal had no idea what he meant.

After a few moments, Alden spoke into his hands through the tears.

"They're ... dead. Mom and Dad are dead, Burly." Addressing it to Burly popped up at the end as one more little coping mechanism, as if by telling Burly he wasn't really telling himself. He couldn't completely own that reality yet.

Finding some additional courage, Alden then spoke more loudly and lifted his face. "Mom and Dad—"

He was startled. Burly was standing right in front of him. Just standing and looking at him. Alden studied his eyes. It wasn't exactly an expression, but they were calm. Surrounded by this mountain of gristled, war-worn hide, Burly's eyes were calm and deep. Alden spoke in a simple tone.

"My parents are dead, Burly." They looked at each other some more, and a slight air of wonder crept into Alden's words. "You know that, don't you. You do. I don't know how you know, but you do, don't you, boy."

Burly huffed a little and let out a low, rumbling groan. It couldn't have been an answer, but it felt like one. Maybe he was just complaining that Alden was stalling.

"Yeah, you're right," said Alden as he stood back up and grabbed his machete. "Let's get moving."

Burly swished around through the foliage and headed back down the path.

It wasn't long before they came up to the water pump. Alden didn't figure this was where Burly was taking him, and he was right. Burly walked on past. Alden wasn't sure if Burly would stop this time if he did, and he sure didn't want to lose him, so Alden skipped the pump business and followed.

Just a few feet later, though, Burly did stop at the spring pond. He stepped up to the edge and put his snout down in the cool, crisp water for a drink. Alden stood next to him and lifted the water bottle out of his pouch.

"Good idea, Burly. Think I'll have some, too." He took a swig.

Burly raised his head and turned it to look at him.

"What?" said Alden.

Burly huffed and put his snout back in the water.

"Oh, I get it. You want me to get some water like you. All right." Alden set his bottle down as he got on his hands and knees at the pond's edge, then bent his face down and scooped some water in his mouth.

"Mmmm ... good water. Now watch." Alden took his bottle and put it in the pond, then lifted it out and drank from it. "See?" He pointed at the bottle. "Water here, too."

Seemingly unimpressed, Burly raised his head again and turned away down the path.

"Well, it's perfectly good water, just like yours," Alden said as he stood again.

Burly wandered on for another ten minutes. Alden thought maybe they were going to the waterfall, put that would take until dark. It was too late in the day for that kind of trek. Then, Burly suddenly veered left and moved into the tall bushes. It was easy for him, but the bushes came back together behind him, and Alden started chopping away with his machete, trying to push ahead as fast as he could.

"Hey! No fair!" Alden said.

He kept hacking away, and after a minute or two, Burly came back and stood, facing him.

"What?" said Alden. "Yeah, I know. I'm not a big monster who can plow through this stuff."

Burly let out a grunt, then, to Alden's complete surprise, lowered himself until he was laying on his belly.

Alden chuckled. "You're weird. So, what's this? We're just going to stop here 'cause I can't go as fast as you?"

Burly tossed his head up a little and grunted again.

"What am I supposed to do? Go around you? I don't even know where I'm going." Alden took a hack at a bush at his side.

More insistent, Burly moaned loudly for a moment, then tossed his head again with a grunt.

"Look, I can't get through here like you. Unless you want to carry me, you'll have to ... oh, wow." An exciting realization came over Alden. "That's it. You want me to ... ride you. Oh, wow."

Alden was enthused at the prospect, and quickly made his way next to the back of Burly's head, where the plate started. "Let's see here," he said as he lifted a foot and tried to find a place to put it. "Hope I don't hurt you."

Burly's bone plate was not attached to his head, but it was close enough that Alden could step near the base of it and use the back of Burly's head to keep from sliding off.

"Here goes." Alden was trying to find a place to grab, and he could reach the dull points at the top of the plate, but needed both hands and couldn't hold very well with his machete. He put that in his teeth, grabbed, and shoved with his leg to propel himself over the top of the plate and onto Burly's back.

"Haha!" he said through the machete. He situated himself, scooting around a little until he was facing forward, one leg on either side of Burly, with the top ridge of the plate right in front of him. The plate came just over his legs, and the points gave him something to hold on to.

He took the machete out of his mouth. "All right, Burly—let's go!"

As if on command, Burly swayed up and back on his legs. It threw Alden around a bit, but he held on.

Burly turned around and slowly started back in the direction he'd been headed, with the bushes parting to either side.

"Holy cannoli. This ... is ... absolutely awesome!" said Alden. "You are unbelievable, boy."

Alden could not get the smile off his face as they rambled through the brush. This was all just preposterous. In a matter of an hour, he had gone from being curious about possibly getting close to this extraordinary animal, to riding its back through the dense forest. It was crazy. It was incredible.

On Burly's back, Alden was a full eight feet off the ground, swaying back and forth with the movements of this fantastic beast. He felt like a character straight out of a movie, or perhaps a game where figuring out you had to ride the animal was the only way into the forest and on to the next level. Every moment of this was a new thrill.

They went on for another twenty minutes or so, with Alden making light comments here and there that Burly ignored, then Alden noticed that the foliage was slowly changing. There were fewer of the dense, woody bushes and more of a different type. They did have a wood structure, but the leaves weren't as small. They were broad and thick, and the bushes themselves were more like umbrellas, spaced farther apart.

After another quarter mile, the forest floor was almost nothing but these new plants. From his height, Alden looked across acres and acres of them. Burly stopped. Alden could see it was easier to stand in these broadleaf bushes, and he swung his left leg over Burly's neck plate and slid down off his right side. Standing within the bushes, the leaves were at Alden's shoulders.

He gave Burly a pat on the side as he looked around. "Thanks, boy."

Burly quickly began eating one of the leaves.

Alden stepped forward near Burly's head. "You like these, Burly?"

He turned his head and looked at Alden for a moment, then went back to eating.

"I don't remember seein' these before," Alden said. "We still had a lot of exploring to do, but it's funny we never saw these. There sure are a lot of 'em."

Burly turned his head again, a little farther this time. He touched his snout to Alden's pouch, then went back to eating.

"What is it, boy? You want me to pick some of these? Oh, wait, I get it. I shared my treat from my pouch, and now you're sharing yours. That's pretty clever. All right." Alden was fascinated by what Burly had done, but moreover, it was not lost on him how important it could be if there were edible plants already growing wildly on the plateau. His parents hadn't analyzed anything yet that looked like a crop, so Alden had no idea if anything was edible. Burly was all the analysis he needed, though. If Burly could eat things, he was willing to bet that he could. He knew there was a risk, of course, but it was his only indicator.

Alden picked a leaf off one of the plants. It was about as big as his hand. "Here goes." He took a bite out of it. It was a little tangy, and a little sweet. For being a green leaf, it tasted a lot like a mild fruit. Alden liked fruit.

"You know what, Burly, this isn't half bad. Now we'll just see if it makes me sick." He polished off the leaf he was eating and took another one. "Might as well go all the way. I think we're gonna spend a lot of time living off these, boy. They better work."

Alden placed a hand on Burly's snout and rubbed gently. "Yup. Nice treat. Thanks, boy." He chewed a moment, then continued. "Well, since we never saw these—" he paused to swallow—"we never named 'em, either. They taste a little fruity, so I think we'll call these ... fruitleaf bushes."

Two of the leaves were enough for now. For Alden, anyway. Burly polished off several more than that while Alden was eating and talking. Alden picked three more leaves and put them in his pouch.

"That should do it," he said, patting his stomach. "Let's go back." He had no idea of where to go now. He didn't really care very much. He had his ravine reconnaissance mission, but he didn't hardly want to go back to that yet. Maybe Burly could help him. Burly could just walk around the ravine edge way faster than Alden could hack a path. That was all for later, though. There would be many days available for doing what he needed to do. Right now, he wasn't planning on anything but riding around with his new friend.

Alden didn't give any thought to how to communicate with Burly that he wanted to ride again. He just stepped back to Burly's shoulder and gave him a pat. Just like it was old business, Burly lowered himself down so Alden could get a foothold like he did before. Machete in his teeth, Alden grabbed, stepped, and pushed up like last time, over Burly's neck plate and onto his back.

As Burly rose again, Alden said, "We've got some things to work on here. First, I need some kind of sling for this stupid machete, and second, I need an easier way up here. Don't know how we'll do that yet, but all this getting down and up is not gonna work. Oh, well. Where to now, Burly Boy?"

Burly started walking and made a curve to his left, which was back south toward the thinner part of the forest. Alden watched as the fruitleaf bushes slowly turned back into the stouter brush, then began to thin into the tall ferns. Alden commented here and there, but was really content to ride along and just look at everything from the perspective of Burly's back. It was wonderful.

They reached the area of the low vine floor, and Burly kept going. Alden could have gotten down and walked by now, but there was no point to that, and a lot less fun. Burly was a little faster walking than Alden, and if Burly was going to come this way, why should they both be on their feet, with Alden needing to hurry the whole time? Riding was way better.

They covered the vine floor part of the forest, and were coming up on the tree line, but they were headed right for the middle of the garden. It was a little ways in front yet, but Alden didn't want Burly to walk through it, so he tried to do something to steer him. He reached down with his right hand and patted near Burly's shoulder.

"I think we need to veer right here, buddy," he said.

Burly didn't alter course at all. "Take a right here, Burly, pal," said Alden. No change. Alden tossed the machete down, flipped his left leg over, and slid down Burly's right side, rolling on the ground when he landed. Burly came to a halt, and Alden got up and trotted around in front of him.

"Look. We need some signals here," Alden said, looking Burly in the eyes. "Sometimes, we can go where you want, but sometimes, we need to go where I want, OK? Now, here's how it's gonna work." He patted his left leg, meaning to Burly's right. "When I pat over here, you go that way, OK?" He waved both his arms that direction. "You go that way. Here, wait a minute."

Alden ran to Burly's side and patted where he had patted while he was riding, then ran back in front. "That means—" he waved his arms again—"you go that way. When I pat over here," he said as he ran to the other side. He patted the other shoulder, ran back to face Burly again, and waved in the other direction. "You go this way."

As he was doing that, he got an idea for a third command. He patted both hands on both legs. "When I pat both hands, that means stop." He held both palms up toward Burly's face. "Stop."

He dropped both hands and let out a sigh. "I sure hope some of this is getting through. All right, let's try it." Burly must have gotten at least some of it, because this time, as Alden walked toward his side, Burly got down for him to mount. "Thanks, Burly."

Once they were moving again, Alden tried his new signals. "OK, boy, here we go. Turn left." He patted Burly's left shoulder, and it worked like a charm. Burly veered a little to his left.

"Yes! Yes! Now right." Alden patted Burly's right shoulder, and he responded.

"Wonderful! One more now." He patted both hands.

"Stop, Burly. Stop."

Burly slowed to a halt. Laughing with delight, Alden slid down again and ran to Burly's head. He threw his arms around the back of it, just in front of the plate, with his face resting right on top of his head. The leathery, dirt-smelling skin was something less than huggable, but Alden was oblivious. "Thank you, Burly. Thank you. You're the best!"

They were close enough to the garden now that Alden figured he'd just lead Burly around it himself on foot. He picked up his machete and walked off to the right, waving for Burly to follow. "This way, buddy." Alden was intentionally leading him to the opposite end as the water pipe and valves, as he didn't want to deal with teaching Burly to step over them, even though it seemed he would have had to already in his travels alone.

Burly moved along with him, and as they were nearing the garden, Alden stood at the corner and stretched out his arms. "Not here. Don't walk in here." Burly came up and stopped. Alden mimicked almost-stepping in the garden by lifting his leg above it, and he shook his head.

"No. Bad."

Then he exaggerated his walk around the edge of the garden and waved with his arms in the proper path. "This way. This is how we walk around the garden. Come on."

Burly followed. When they were clear of the garden, Alden raised his hands.

"Stop." Burly did. "You are so awesome," Alden said as he walked around to Burly's side. "Now we can go wherever you want."

Burly let Alden mount again, then began walking. They did go wherever Burly wanted, but it was going to change Alden's plans in a way he would never expect of himself.

Chapter 10

Past the edge of the garden and into the open rock, Burly plodded along with Alden on his back. Alden was curious where Burly could have wanted to go out here, since there wasn't any food, and nothing to see except the burned house and Alden's cave. Maybe Burly hadn't been in the rocky part of the plateau yet and just wanted to explore.

They were only a couple hundred feet from the edge of the ravine, and rather than make his way out toward the middle of the open terrain, Burly was angling slightly closer and closer to the edge. Before long, it seemed apparent he was headed for what was left of the bridge. Alden was wondering if he'd been there before.

"Have you been on the bridge, boy?" he asked. "It's not there anymore, but maybe you know that already, too. Did you come all the way across the bridge?"

Burly kept on until they came right up to the base of it, and he stopped while facing across the ravine. He raised his head slightly and let out a tremendous, deep, mournful wail that was far louder than anything Alden had heard come out of him before. It was a cry of pain, made more somber by the reverberations lingering from the ravine, as if it empathized.

Alden slid down Burly's left side and stood next to his head, looking down at the buggy in the ravine. "Yes, Burly," he said softly. "I lost my Dad down there."

Burly once again called out with a bellowing lament. This time, after the echoes from the ravine faded away, Alden heard the sound again, faintly in the distance. It was from far away in the grassland. Alden had thought plenty about his own family, but had not yet considered anything about Burly's. This was a revelation.

"Oh, my gosh," said Alden. "There's more of you over there, isn't there. You've got a family over there." He put a hand on Burly's head. "You came across the bridge and got stuck here." He paused. "There's no secret path to get on or off the plateau here, is there, Burly. You're not supposed to be here at all. And you wouldn't be if we didn't build that bridge."

Alden thought for a moment. He looked again at the buggy in the ravine, and thought about family. About how he would feel if it were his parents calling to him from the grassland, and how he would do anything, whatever it took, to get to them. He walked out onto the short bit of remaining bridge, turned, and faced Burly.

"Burly, I'm sorry about you bein' stuck here. I never thought about it that way before. I thought you could come and go, and I could find out how. I'm sorry. My mom and dad are gone, and I think you know that, but now I know that *your* family isn't gone." He pointed behind him. "They're over there." He stepped forward and put his hand on Burly's snout.

"Well, here's the way it is. The only chance I could ever have to get off this planet is if I get over there and see what happened at the Grass Camp. The only chance you could ever have to see your family again is if you get over there, too. So, here's what we're gonna do. We're gonna go over there. We're gonna figure out a way to build something we can get across on. Both of us, Burly. We're gonna build a bridge. I don't know how, or how long it'll take, but that's what we're gonna do. We're gonna go home. Both of us. That's a promise, boy."

Alden turned around and looked across the ravine. The sun was getting low, and he needed more food and water. He had fruitleaves in his pouch for that, but Burly must be needing some, too. For today, it was time to think about getting some rest; for tomorrow, his mind was racing as he pondered how to begin this exciting and monumental task of rebuilding a bridge across the ravine. It could be done. It must be done. He felt it even more for Burly than he did for himself. Everyone Alden knew already thought he was dead; if he actually died, the universe would be no different. Everyone Burly knew was waiting for him. Alden had no idea how burlons lived or what their society was like, but Burly's forlorn trumpeting of anguish and the answer that came back from deep in the grassland was all he needed to know. Burly had to get home.

Alden awoke in his cave with a renewed sense of purpose. The day before, he'd had a plan, too, but this one was different. Yesterday's plan was about finding his own way; today's plan was about working together with his new friend, toward a common goal. It was a daunting task, one that he had no real idea how to accomplish. It was also a task with a much longer timeline. Before, he was just going to find how Burly got onto the plateau and leave the same way; now, he was looking at weeks and weeks of work. And yet, the new plan was more exciting and filled him with expectations of discovery with Burly.

Even so, he was going to have to get used to dealing with the fact that daily living was its own huge challenge. He needed a change of clothes. The ones he was wearing and the ones still in the ravine down by the stream from last time all needed washing. He needed to pull and wash more carrots, to make sure he kept using them so none would go to waste. He needed to tend to the rest of the garden, too, to keep up with weeding and checking the condition of the other crops. He needed to turn off the water pump, like he was going to yesterday. *Then*, he needed to figure out how to build a bridge.

Alden was trying to prepare himself for the mental drudgery of understanding that every day was going to be like that for a very, very long time. Food plans, water plans, gardening, washing, staying alive. He tried to project what it would be like and muster his resolve to stick to it, and that was better than not, but he had no real idea what kind of toll surviving on his own for any length of time was going to take.

Part of the food plan was the cans he saved. Thirty-seven of them. Having no concept of what it would take to build a bridge, he had to think in terms of staying alive indefinitely, and that would include using the cans all up by the time they started going bad.

The freshness dates on them varied but the longest ones were roughly two years out. To make it a little easier to figure, Alden used one hundred weeks to estimate how often he could eat something from a can, then divided by thirty-seven. That was pretty dismal. One can every nineteen days. Almost three weeks.

Besides being too hard to keep track of, eating only one can every three weeks sounded more depressing than none at all. Alden decided to just eat the cans up however he wanted and deal with living off the land. As far as long-term survival was concerned, his cans were pretty much not a factor.

It did occur to him, though, that he was already losing track in his head of how many days he'd been on his own. Part of him really didn't care. That part said living was living, and he'd just take every day as it came. But he could also tell he would feel a trifle unsettled by not knowing. He realized with a little intrigue that there was something basic about understanding what day it was, something that provided a reference to normality. The machete had a curved portion of the blade out near the end, and he took it to one end of his supply log, where he made five notches. He wasn't sure what he'd do later, if anything, about organizing a calendar out of it, but at least he had a count. Without real certainty, he was nevertheless reasonably confident this was day five. Five days since his birthday. From here, at least, he would know for sure.

Regardless of counting days, though, he still wasn't interested in stringing out or tracking his consumption of cans, so he dug into a delicious breakfast of salmon, then climbed out of the cave to get started.

It was a sunny, breezy day. Not nearly as windy as the day he saved all his cans and clothing, but breezier than normal. Burly was nowhere to be seen. Burly had accompanied Alden to his cave the evening before, but obviously wandered away to his own business once Alden was inside.

Alden didn't pack any clothes with him; he figured he'd wear the ones in the ravine once he washed them. He left the machete in the cave and opted instead for his hatchet, which he could carry in his pouch without damaging it if the blade was facing up. The only other thing in his pouch was a water bottle, but he was carrying the garden hoe he'd found with half the handle. Alden had his path planned out—garden first, to drop off the hoe and pull some carrots; out to the bridge to climb down to the stream and wash himself, his clothes, and the carrots; into the forest to turn off the water pump; then on to find Burly and start figuring out how to be a bridge engineer.

When he got to the garden, he took a look around at how things were growing. The lettuce had already been harvested right at the end of the rainy season, so that was gone for good. The beans were going strong and would start to come in after another few weeks, and the carrots he already knew were ready to pick. They had corn, but that was just starting. He remembered how his parents had chuckled about having the extra month in the year and how that meant the corn should be "knee high by the fourth of Arido."

It wasn't yet a full month after the rainy season, and even though they wouldn't typically have used the irrigation yet, there hadn't been any follow-on showers, and Alden was about to shut off the water pump. He decided he'd best douse the garden well; once now and once on his way back through to the forest path and the pump.

He pulled the valve open and let the water gush out into the garden. Any other time, this was a play session. He'd be in the torrent, getting soaked and dirty, then washing off and doing it again. Today, it just didn't seem like the right thing to do. He wasn't ready to make any memories like that without Dad and Mom around. He'd already had the adventure of his life with Burly, and he would never be able to share that with them, but that was different. That experience was totally separate from his parents. Playing in the irrigation tube was too close to them. It wasn't right. Not yet.

After another couple of minutes, the shallow ditches

between the crop rows were full, and Alden shut off the valve. He wandered down the carrot row to where he'd pulled the last ones, got on a knee, and started working some more of them out of the soil. It was a little easier now that the dirt was wet. He pulled eight—enough to split with Burly—and put them in his pouch. There were maybe fifty left, not counting the twenty more that were supposed to go to seed.

As he stood, Alden heard noises from the forest. It was Burly, coming across the forest floor.

"Hey, there, boy!" said Alden as he skipped a step and launched a spirited walk toward him. When they met, Alden patted a hand on the top of Burly's snout. "Mornin', Burly. How ya doin'?" Burly let out a huff and a grunt.

"You must've known I was pickin' carrots, huh. Here, have a couple." Alden pulled two out of his pouch and held them near Burly's mouth in his open palm. Burly took them, and Alden could feel Burly's rough lips, smooth teeth, and wet tongue, but Burly bit nothing but carrot.

"Yeah, that's the way," said Alden. "I've gotta get washed up and stuff, but as long as you're here already, there's something I wanna try. I've been thinkin' about how we're gonna need some kind of rope if we're gonna build a bridge. Prob'ly a lot of it. And the only stuff around to use for that is these vines."

Alden started looking around in the thicket of old, dead vines beneath them. "Most of these really old ones here are prob'ly too weak, but ... " He grabbed one that was very stiff, then let go and grabbed another one that was a little more pliable. Flowing from the trees, the vines were a deep green. Once they had fallen, they turned brown, then a dark grey. Like the trees themselves, the vines got stronger as they dried out, but also eventually got brittle. Alden had found a brown one that was still somewhat pliable but resilient. It was about twelve feet long, a quarter-inch thick at one end and tapered thinner at the other. Near the thin end, he wrapped a loop of it around each hand, which was difficult from the stiffness; he wouldn't have been able to do that at the thicker end. He tugged and tugged on it between his hands, but couldn't break it.

"Perfect."

Next, he took the two ends and managed to wrangle a knot, mostly using the thin end, but he got it secure enough that he couldn't pull the knot off the thick end.

"There we go. Now, watch this, Burly Boy."

Alden stepped behind Burly's neck plate on his right side, took his loop of vine, and flung it up over Burly, without letting go. The first two attempts didn't do what he wanted, but the third one did. He got the vine hooked on one of the top points of Burly's neck plate, and when he pulled down on it, the loop came down to just above his knee, with both strands of the vine behind the plate.

"That's it." Alden reached up with a foot and placed it in the loop, then gently began to put weight on it. "Is that OK, boy?" Burly didn't respond, but he also hadn't gotten down on the ground for Alden to climb on, which he always had by this time if Alden was by his side.

Alden smoothly lifted himself until all his weight was on the vine loop, testing both the strength of the vine and Burly's reaction.

"You OK, boy?" This time, Burly grunted.

"All right, then." Alden lowered himself back down, then, grabbing a nearby plate point with his hand, he used the vine loop like a stirrup to propel himself up onto Burly's back.

"Yes! That's the way," Alden said with delight. "We're on our way, Burly. To the bridge!" He gave a little kick with his feet, which he hadn't tried before, and Burly started walking ahead toward the garden.

Right away, Alden gave Burly a pat on his left shoulder. He wanted to see how Burly would handle stepping over the water pipe. Burly veered to the left, and stayed on that course for a bit, but as he got closer to the pipe he started angling to walk alongside it. Alden tapped Burly's left shoulder again.

"It's OK, boy," he said. "Let's see how you do getting over the water pipe."

The pipe was laying on the ground, ten inches high. Burly came up and stepped right over it, fairly nimbly. His belly cleared without scraping, but not by a lot.

"Terrific," said Alden. "Now we can move around this end of the garden without you plowin' right through it."

Alden guided Burly past the garden and out into the open rock, then to the bridge. He slid down off Burly's back and came around to give his snout a little rub.

"Got some business to take care of in the ravine, buddy. You can wait if you want, but you won't hurt my feelings if you want to go back to the forest. Your choice."

With that, Alden walked to the bridge ladder and climbed down. He took off his clothes, grabbed the others that were still there, and took them all to the water. One by one, he rinsed and rubbed everything until he figured it was as clean as he was likely to get it. He rubbed himself down, too, and the carrots he brought. He was anxious to get to his bridge plans, but he also knew he would need to discipline himself to do proper chores, and he took his time about it.

When he finished, he put on his wet clothes from before—cherry-stained khaki shorts and a green T-shirt with game warrior Thalok on it—and took a few minutes to wander around the ravine and see if anything down there gave him ideas. There was quite a bit of twisted metal, and four large, round wooden footings that were the base of the primary supports for the demolished bridge. None of it sparked any thoughts on how to make use of it, though, as he couldn't find anything straight or long enough to stand all the way up to the bridge height anymore. Still, it was good to take an inventory of what he had at his disposal. It was a lot of material if he could just figure out a way to use it.

Chapter 11

Alden made his way across the ravine until he was at the base of the opposite wall. He looked up the sheer rock face and thought it felt so close. Right up there was the grassland. So close he could literally smell it; the grassland had a grainy aroma, and it wafted down into the ravine. If he could just get up that wall, this would all be over. He could get to the Grass Camp, call for help, and ECOP could get Burly across the ravine. All he had to do was get up that cliff.

A moment later, he thought through it some more and realized that even taking advantage of an opportunity to climb that wall, if he ever had one, would be risky. He had no idea what shape the Grass Camp was in. If it was completely demolished, he'd have nowhere else better to go and might not have a way to get himself back down into the ravine to get back to Burly, depending on how he'd gotten up there.

Plus, he would have far fewer resources. There were some trees at the north end of the grassland, but not brushtops. No vines to make rope out of. And he didn't know where the water was. All in all, if you were going to be stuck on Cappa Terse, the plateau was the place to be. Once the new bridge was built, even if the Grass Camp was useless, he could still get back and live in the forest and his cave.

Still, if he could somehow get himself up that wall, and by some stroke of luck get a radio signal out at the Grass Camp, that would be far too valuable in saving the enormous time and effort of building a bridge. There was just no way to do it. Not that he could think of. If he could tip a brushtop to lean, he could possibly climb up, but he had no method of standing up a tree. Even if he could, the tree would be almost vertical, so he'd have to shimmy all the way up, and any tipping when he was near the top would be a disaster.

He also thought of possibly throwing something up that could catch and hold, but that couldn't work, either. Alden barely had enough strength to throw a small rock up there, and no chance at all to do it with the weight of a vine attached. Besides, there was nothing up there but the smooth, gently tapered rock edge, and some grass. Nothing to grip. The tantalizing edge above him remained so close, yet impossible to reach.

Alden made his way back across the ravine, stepping over bent angle-iron braces and through the stream. He donned his pouch, now toting a hatchet, some clean carrots, a bottle of water, and a washed set of clothes. When he arrived back at the top of the ladder, he'd been gone for some time; he was pleased to see that Burly was still there, lying down in the sun. With Burly's size and thick skin, Alden would have thought maybe he'd prefer to spend his time in shade, but then he remembered burlons live in the grassland, and shade was sparse. Burly was used to the sun.

"Hey, boy," said Alden as he walked up.

Burly started to rise, but wasn't able to get all the way up before he was jostled to the ground again.

The ground was moving.

It shook and shifted an inch or two, and Alden and Burly were both taken completely by surprise. Alden kept his balance at first. It didn't dawn on him that the open rock was already the safest possible place to be in an earthquake, and he reacted purely on instinct to head for cover.

"Come on, boy!" said Alden as he took off running for the forest.

Burly was less anxious, and was making no attempt to stand again while there was no footing. Alden made it ten steps before the ground lurched and he turned an ankle, tumbling over on the hard surface.

As he bounced around, he pulled his left knee up and held it to his chest, yelling out in pain. A moment later he decided being in a ball was too unstable, and he put his arms and legs out to minimize movement.

Alden and Burly both lay on the surging rock for another half-minute as the quake subsided. When it seemed safe to move, they both started to stand, but Alden was having trouble putting weight on his left foot.

"You OK, Burly?" he asked. "You all right?"

Burly was righting himself spryly as Alden hopped toward him, gingerly testing his injured ankle.

"Well, that was new. Holy cannoli."

Burly came to meet him, and Alden put a hand on his neck plate to steady himself.

"You look like you're doing OK. That's good. I hurt my ankle."

Alden continued to test it as Burly made some light, low groaning noises.

"Never seen an earthquake up here before, Burly. Hope they don't happen very often."

He took his hand off Burly's plate and tried to walk. The pain was sharp, but it was already less than when he first hurt it. He could feel it starting to swell over the top of his tennis shoe.

"Looks like I'm not gonna be walkin' very good for a while, boy. Last time this happened, Mom wrapped it up and put ice on it. Don't have ice, but I can get it wrapped up, I think. Let's go to the cave and see what's there."

The vine stirrup Alden had slung over Burly's plate was still hanging there, as was his intention when he made it. He held onto a plate point with both hands to take the weight off his bad ankle while he got his good one up and into the stirrup, then he could launch himself onto Burly's back. Burly started walking immediately, and Alden steered him toward his cave.

When they got there, Alden climbed in and looked around. Things were a little disheveled from the earthquake, but nothing alarming, and he sorted through the clothing he had to see what might work. He found one long-sleeved shirt of Dad's, which was perfect. It had a light tan and green checkered pattern on it, and given the climate on Cappa Terse, it was probably the only long-sleeved shirt they'd even had in the house, but there it was. Sitting on his flat log, he twirled the body of the shirt around itself until the whole thing was one length of fabric from cuff to cuff. He removed his shoe and sock, and passed the shirt around his ankle and foot several times before tying it together.

Alden stood and tested it. It was bulky, but it did give him some support. He was going to have to be careful for a while, but at least he could get around with some limping. He wouldn't need crutches, something that would have laid him up completely. Putting a shoe on over the bandage was impossible, but Alden didn't see that as a big deal. The sole of his foot beneath the instep was protected, and that was plenty.

Burly was waiting for him as Alden reached the surface again.

"All fixed up, boy," said Alden, showing Burly his wrapped ankle. "Let's go figure out how to build a bridge." He hobbled up to grab the vine stirrup and paused.

"Oh, wait. I almost forgot." He moved to Burly's head as he pulled a couple of carrots out of his pouch. "Anybody who survives an earthquake ought to get a carrot treat, at least." He held them out to Burly, who quickly snatched them and began munching. Alden patted his snout.

"You're a good boy, Burly," he said. "The best. Anybody can have a cat or a dog. Not me. I have a burlon, and you're the best buddy ever. You and me, we're gonna beat this thing, Burly. We're gonna do this. We're the heroes of Cappa Terse, and we're gonna get back where we belong."

Alden was never sure exactly how much Burly understood of what he was saying. As far as language itself, he presumed Burly knew nothing, but the way Burly acted and looked at him made him wonder. Burly really was an amazing animal, and that made it easier for Alden to talk to him the way he needed to talk to someone. Even if Burly knowing what he meant was just pretend, he was another thinking, feeling, listening being, and that meant everything.

In the state Alden's thoughts were swirling, having Burly was life-saving. Alden was in a constantly tumultuous world of despair, excitement, and bewilderment, and Burly was his place to focus, his reason for staying sane. For staying alive.

"All right, boy, let's hit the forest."

Alden climbed aboard and snacked on a carrot himself as they wandered toward the trees. Alden hadn't forgotten that his first destination was supposed to be to turn off the water pump, and he guided Burly that direction. On the way, they stopped at the irrigation valve to flood the garden one more time before the water was shut down, then they continued into the woods and down the path.

The earthquake hadn't seemed to change anything. They followed along the pipe as they went, and Alden didn't see any leaks or other problems. The only thing he noticed about the forest was that the shaking had rustled more of the floral scent from the brushtops, the way a windy day did.

"Well, let's see what we've got here," Alden said as they arrived at the pump. He stood next to the whirring machine and looked it over, hoping this would be fairly simple. He was not disappointed. From the solar panels on top, which were above Alden's height, small tubes came down the side to a metal box about eighteen inches square. It had a latch at the bottom and hinges on top.

"This better be it," said Alden, flipping the latch. He lifted the door and saw two round, plastic buttons slightly recessed inside metal cylinders designed to prevent accidental pushing. One was red, the other green. To one side was a six-inch, vertical lever with a red knob on the end. It was in the upper position, labeled "ON." Above it read "Master Power."

Alden pointed to the lever. "Think we'll leave that one alone, eh, boy?" He turned to look back at Burly as if for acknowledgement, but Burly was already starting to move along to the spring pond for a drink.

"Oh. Yeah. Good idea, boy. Help yourself."

Alden turned his attention back to the control box. The green and red plastic buttons were labeled "Run" and

"Stop." Alden pushed the red button, and the whirring sounds swiftly slowed to a single click, then nothing.

"All right," said Alden. "I think that's it. Now we just hope the green one gets us back up and running when we need water."

Alden hobbled down to the spring pond as he took his water bottle out of the pouch and downed a big gulp. He refilled it in the pond and stood up again, then turned and faced across the path, looking at the bushes opposite the pond. Their stems and branches were thick enough to make stout sticks.

"Well, Burly, old pal," he said, "I hate to say it, but I don't know how to build a bridge. We didn't quite cover that in any of my books or nothin'. We're gonna figure this out, though. Got to. But here's the thing. There's nothin' from the old bridge left to use. It's blasted to smithereens. We're gonna have to chop down a bunch of these trees to build a bridge. It's the only way." He limped across the path as he put his water bottle into his pouch and took out his hatchet. "But we can't just cut down trees and dump them into the ravine and hope they turn into a bridge. We need a plan, boy. We need a model. Mom and Dad always planned. 'If you fail to plan, you plan to fail,' they said. I'm going to have to figure out how to stand the trees up and tie them together so they stay that way."

Alden hacked a couple of the bushes down and started stripping the branches, then paused.

"Think I'll need to sit down for this."

He chopped a couple more bushes and hobbled off back toward the clearer area of the forest, where he could find a fallen log to sit on. Burly followed along closely, almost nudging him. Alden got the feeling he was asking if Alden needed a ride. Alden could see a downed tree among the lower fern plants and decided he could get there on his own.

"Not this time, Burly. Thanks, but I only need to get to that tree."

He limped over to it and sat. He swung the hatchet several times in front of him to clear a working space in the brush, then set down the bushes he'd cut. He ripped the branches off and stripped the leaves, then broke or chopped the sticks and twigs into lengths of six inches or so. Once he had a pile of about twenty of those, he began assembling them into trial structures, to see what would stay standing and what wouldn't.

His first several attempts fell over almost instantly. Some others stood until he put a little pressure down on them, then they twisted or collapsed. He made some round forms like teepees, and those stood well, but he couldn't see how he would use those easily for a long structure like a bridge.

Alden stood to stretch himself. Burly had been hanging around patiently, but Alden knew this was still going to take some time.

"You should go on and do whatever you need to do," said Alden. Burly gave his head a little toss and grunted. Alden limped over to him and placed a hand on his snout.

"I'm fine. I'm just workin' on our bridge. This is the idea phase. The planning phase. I wish I could do it faster, but that's just the way things are. Sometimes it's not going to make sense for you to just wait for me. Go get some lunch from the fruitleaf bushes and I'll be fine here. Honest."

Burly tossed his head again.

"Really, boy, it's OK." He waved his hand. "Go on ahead. You must need more food and water. Go ahead, boy."

Alden shuffled away toward his log. Burly paused, then turned and headed off into the brush toward the deep forest. Alden thought some more, had some water and a carrot, and sat back down to keep building and testing.

He tried a couple more things that weren't very robust or would take far too many trees to be practical. Eventually, he began to realize he was not going to be able to make a reliable structure solely by leaning or resting trees against each other. He was going to have to create connections and joints by tying trees together. He started tying thin bits of vine around some joints.

That seemed promising, but everything he tried was still terribly wobbly. He tried to think about how the metal bridge was built, and he remembered that it wasn't just vertical posts holding everything up. There were other bars at an angle between the posts. Maybe that was important. It took hours, but angled braces helped immensely, and at long last Alden was constructing a frame he could push down on and not easily crush. He continued with another section of the same design, bracing and tying and pushing. The whole thing stayed standing and couldn't be wiggled back and forth or squashed easily.

"Burly!" said Alden. "I think I've got it!" He rose to his feet and put his arms in the air. "I've got it! We can build a bridge!"

Burly was too far away to respond immediately, but that did not dampen Alden's enthusiasm.

"All right," said Alden to no one in particular, "we need trees." He clapped his hands together. "Lots of trees and lots of vines." He started looking around at the trees in his area, as if sizing them up like he'd never examined them before. "I don't want to use anything that's been on the forest floor a while, but if I chop something down, we'll have fresh wood and fresh vines."

He limped over to a nearby brushtop. The one he was sitting on was still reasonably close to the spring pond path, and he didn't want to chop anything that might fall on the path or the water pipeline, so he moved further into the woods and chose a likely suspect with a trunk roughly two feet in diameter.

"Yeah, here we go." He grabbed his hatchet and held it with both hands. He'd been swinging it around already at the smaller shrubs, but this time it felt different. He felt more like a man, doing something a man needed to do. Alden lifted it back and swung it forward on a horizontal arc at his waist.

The blade embedded about a quarter-inch into the flesh of the tree. Alden had pictured something closer to slicing cleanly through, although he certainly knew better than to expect that. It was just the image in his head.

"All right," he said, exhaling heavily. He pulled the hatchet out of the wood and dealt another mighty blow.

This one landed several inches away from the first, and the blade was not straight, so on impact it didn't really do any damage at all. It just flipped around out of Alden's hands and landed in the ferns. It stung a little, too.

"Ow." Alden instinctively shook his hands around and flexed his fingers from the sensation.

"Well, OK. Let's think about this."

He did, and as he thought, he realized that no matter how many trees he was going to eventually use, they were all going to need to get moved to the bridge area. In his fervor, he had started on any old tree, but realistically, it was a silly tree to be chopping. He was still right near the spring pond, probably two miles from the bridge. That was crazy.

"Right," he said. Burly was nowhere in sight, but Alden was still speaking out loud, mostly out of habit from talking to Burly. There was no harm in it; if anything, he'd want Burly to hear him whenever he was close again. So in a way, he wasn't talking to himself; he was making sure Burly would be able to hear anything as soon as he was near enough.

Alden parted the ferns at his feet, retrieved his hatchet, and started limping away toward the southern edge of the forest, near the garden. He considered calling out to Burly before he left; he really felt companionship when Burly was around. But he also knew that he didn't own Burly, and even if Burly would come—and he probably would—if Burly needed more eating and drinking and wandering, he should have it. He was a wild animal, after all. It was anyone's guess what a burlon does with his free time.

After twenty minutes, Alden was thinking it might not have been a good idea to do all that walking on his bad ankle. It was hurting more. His open heel and toes weren't a problem; he enjoyed spending time barefoot, especially in the open rock, so his soles weren't tender. The ankle was, though, and Alden decided to find another fallen brushtop to rest on.

He sat facing the deeper forest, mostly so he could see if Burly came following him. He drank some water and bit into his last clean carrot, thinking he would rather be enjoying one of his canned foods. Even the vegetables. He cautioned himself that it was pretty early in his solitary life on the plateau to be sick of eating something, but he couldn't deny it. He was just going to have to live with it. When crops were ready to eat, they needed to be eaten. A month from now, he'd probably really wish he had carrots.

Thinking of getting fed up with food options brought another thought to mind, one he hadn't spent much time with yet—fire. Even if all he had to cook were plants, hot food suddenly sounded magnificent.

Every couple of months, he and his folks had enjoyed an outdoor campfire. Dad showed him how to get it started, but there were matches. He knew the construction concept, with kindling under larger twigs under larger ones, then logs, all the while keeping the heat in the center and not smothering it with tightly packed wood. He just didn't have the spark; he knew there were ways to make heat and start a flame, but Dad hadn't gotten that far. He'd have to think on that. Maybe there was something in one of the books that escaped the house fire. Ironically, he realized he would now consider it a good thing if part of that were still burning.

A sound came from the deep forest. Rustling and rumbling. It had to be Burly, but he wasn't walking. In a few seconds, Burly came out of the bushes in the distance. He was in a dead run toward Alden.

Alden stood, in case this meant something was wrong or Burly was being chased, but before long it seemed apparent he was just running to run. He made quite a racket, slashing through bushes and pounding the ground with those tree-trunk legs. A galloping burlon was a remarkable sight, right out of the movies. Alden imagined a battle scene with armored warriors astride dozens of thundering burlons, then imagined himself there, feeling the immense power in the rumble beneath his feet.

He still couldn't believe he was actually friends with a beast like this.

Burly slowed as he approached Alden, walking the last fifty feet while he huffed and slobbered and caught his breath.

"Gettin' some exercise, boy?" asked Alden.

Burly came right up to him, and Alden reached to lay a hand on his snout as he often did, but Burly was a bit too fidgety for that yet.

"Wow. That was some sprint. I better let you calm down a little."

Alden sat again, and although he didn't really have anything much to do except not hurt his ankle and wait for Burly, his mind was racing with thoughts about how to construct their bridge. He was going to have to do a lot of tying. He'd made quite a few little knots in his model, and in real life those knots would be tied around pairs of two-foot-thick tree trunks.

He was planning to figure out a way to test some things before he actually tried them in the ravine, but he was fairly confident that a single thickness of vine would be much too weak. He could tie very long strings of vines end-to-end, and wrap them many times around the trees in his bridge frame. Or—and this seemed the better choice—he could make ropes out of vines, ropes that were several vines thick already before he went to using them on the bridge. Alden had used regular rope before, and it wasn't like a single cord of material. It was a whole bunch of cords twisted together. Just like with the angle braces on the bridge frame, he wasn't sure why that would be important, but somehow it probably was.

When Alden thought about how this was all going to work, it seemed completely overwhelming, and part of that was imagining how to get himself in a position to tie all the joints in the model of sticks he made. Lots of them weren't on the ground or at the top. Wrapping vines was going to be hard, and doing it as little as he could would make it better. A rope made out of three vines needed to be wrapped around trees only one-third as many times as a single vine would. Five-vine rope, even better.

In any event, he needed gobs of vines, and the best ones to work with were going to be the live ones drooping from the living brushtops. It was time to chop one down and begin the harvest.

Chapter 12

Alden had ridden Burly to the edge of the forest, or near it. He chose a likely tree, one that wasn't as thick as some of the others, and one that wouldn't be able to fall on either the garden or the water pipe. He lifted the hatchet out of his pouch. After a deep breath, Alden dealt his first blow. It was a hit; the blade went into the wood. Not far, but considering his last attempt, he was already learning that less flailing and more concentration on controlling the blade would be a good thing. He needed to be ready to learn how to be very good at this.

Alden took another chop. This one landed true, also, though not very close to the first one. His third hack went awry, with the blade twisting its way out of his hands again. Three times in, and Alden was already getting lax in his concentration. He was surprised at the focus it took, actually. Chopping a tree down never seemed to be a big deal. Not until you tried it. It turned out to be a little more than taking a few swings and yelling, "Timber!"

This was going to be a way of life, though—in more ways than one—and Alden kept at it, trying to pay attention to the right combination of speed and guidance to be able to consistently land the blade while doing the most damage to the tree in the process. Alden was a studier, and also a gamer, and this new skill presented itself as a challenge to both aspects of his personality. He was trying to learn it while he also competed with himself to be better at it, as if chopping a tree down within a certain number of swings earned him a larger hatchet for the next game level.

It was awkward, though. He couldn't maintain his balance well enough on his bad ankle to get the right leverage on his swing. Alden was anxious to get this going, but he had to face facts that it was getting really late in the day and he was very hungry. Chopping down a tree was going to have to wait until the next day.

Burly had been hanging around aimlessly, and Alden went to him to get a ride to his cave. Alden immediately ripped into a delicious can of kidney beans, followed by another of pears. It was heavenly; the fruit was exquisite, and even just the sweet syrup it was canned in was nectar of the gods. After that, Alden looked through the books he had, to find one on camping or survival— something that would give him a clue about starting a fire—but there was nothing like that. It was a mixture of science books and novels. Nothing very helpful.

He lay down for the night, and as he drifted off he got an idea. He needed sunlight, though. Plenty of that to be had the morning.

‹❖›

Alden awoke to find Burly nearby. The day before, Burly had been off doing whatever he does in the forest. Today, he was wandering around the open rock, not far from Alden's cave.

"Mornin', Burly," said Alden as he emerged. Burly sauntered toward him, and Alden met him with a pat on the snout. Alden was in the same clothes—the khaki shorts and green, Thalok T-shirt—sporting Dad's safari hat and his pouch with water and hatchet.

"Hey, boy. New plan today. I don't think I'm going to need you much, but you're welcome to hang around."

Alden's ankle was somewhat better, and part of his new plan for the day was to keep his walking closer to home and let it heal more. He started off toward the burned house with a lighter limp. Burly came alongside.

"I know how we're going to make fire, Burly," Alden said. "Well, I know how I wanna try. Gotta find some stuff first. I had a science kit with stuff in it to run some really cool experiments. Chemicals and stuff. I had a magnifying glass in that kit, and I used to focus the sun with it. I burned my hand once. I bet it would start a fire. Gotta look really hard and see if it's layin' around out here."

The lab had been on the north side of the house, facing the forest, and Alden was walking that way to search the remaining rubble for leftovers. There was still lots of junk that wasn't badly burned, just twisted or smashed, and it didn't make the cut when he was first looking for tools and such. He could easily have not recognized or simply dismissed pieces of his science experiment kit.

As they traveled, Burly occasionally huffed or grunted, for no apparent reason. He did that. Sometimes, Alden just looked over at him and marveled. This animal was a huge, wickedly powerful thing, with his thick, grey-brown mottled skin, thumping legs, and wildly awesome neck plate. He had a smell that was vaguely musky and dirty but made you feel connected to the very planet itself. With all that, he was also smart and graceful, with those strangely kind and knowing eyes.

And the best part was that he actually seemed to want to be Alden's friend. Alden didn't really have to do anything but offer some carrots and show that he was friendly. Burly leapt in from there. Burlons were clearly social among themselves, too; Burly proved that with his mournful cry at the bridge. Maybe humans and burlons were a natural fit. Alden imagined a world on Cappa Terse where both species worked together all the time. And here was Alden, pioneering the relationship that could establish a new bond that lasted far into the future.

But mostly, Burly was really cool to be hanging out with.

"All right, here we are," said Alden as they got closer to the part of the debris field where most of the lab stuff landed. "Keep your eyes peeled for a magnifying glass or a blue and white box."

Alden took a swig of his water and pulled out the hatchet, just to use as a tool to move chunks of debris around and look under them. It was going to be more tedious this time around, but Alden was ready for that. He was in a good frame of mind, a healthy combination of excited anticipation to start on building the bridge and patience to work step by step on things that needed to be done. They were going to want to have fire in their arsenal of survival resources, and today was about the search for fire.

An hour into the hunt, though, Alden was getting a little more restless. He hadn't found anything interesting, and he was moving a little faster. He was less meticulous, and spent more time standing straight up and kicking things out of the way than bending over and looking under them.

Burly was still standing around, but farther out near the edge of the scattered rubble. Alden paused for a drink, and stretched around at the waist. He needed to sit down soon.

"Hey, boy, look at that," Alden said loudly as he pointed to the sky in the southern distance.

There was a bird gliding high in the air, the likes of which Alden had never seen. It was far off, but Alden could tell it was absolutely enormous. Burly came a little closer to Alden, and was facing the bird. He seemed to have noticed the same thing.

"Wow, that thing is huge."

From this distance, the bird looked completely black. As it flew, it was moving toward the east, but it seemed to be curving in an arc. A few moments later, it was in the eastern sky, but the same distance away, and Alden and Burly kept watching as it continued in what became evident as a full loop around the plateau. Not very close to it, but definitely flying in a circle with the rocky area of the plateau in the center.

"What do you think he's doin', boy?" said Alden. "I think that's one of the birds Randy told me about from the Grass Camp. Picked up a whole cat and carried it off. Nothin' for him out here, though. He's a long way from home."

Burly tossed his head a little and let out a grunt.

"Bet you've seen those guys before, huh, Burly. Bet they leave you alone, though."

After another complete circle, the bird flew off to the west, over the grassland.

"That was cool," said Alden. "Wish he'd come a little closer so I could see him."

Burly tossed and grunted again, a little more animated this time.

"What is it, boy? You don't like them, do you? Did he take a little one of yours or somethin'? Is that it? Don't worry, he's gone."

Alden turned his attention back to the sprawling expanse of mangled house bits and looked it over as he thought some more.

"Oh, hey, wait a minute," he said with a sudden idea. "I know what. I don't need my science kit, boy. I saw the microscope over here." He started off with a slight hobble. "It's all broken up, but it has magnifiers in it. If I can get one out, we'll be all set."

Alden made his way to the area where he remembered seeing the microscope parts. Burly followed. Alden turned over a few charred bits of roof.

"Yes! Here we go." Alden picked up an eyepiece, a hard plastic tube three inches long. "This has a lens in it. I think." He held it up to his eye. "Hmmm ... it's got somethin' ... " He turned it around and looked the other direction, then held his hand just past the end.

"Oh, yeah, this is it." Alden looked it over, figuring out how to best attack it to get the lens out. There was a small one at one end, and a larger one at the other. It looked like the best way was to chop it in the middle. He set it down on the rock, took his hatchet, and set the point of the blade down in the center. He didn't trust his aim for taking a swing at it. He placed the heel of his hand on the butt of the hatchet blade and thrust down. The eyepiece squirted out and shot across the ground.

Alden gave out a little yelp as he chased it down, but he found it again quickly and tried another approach. This time, he held one end of the piece and took the hatchet in his other hand, gently tapping at the center of the tube with increasing strokes. After a few, he got brave enough to take a larger swing, and the tube shattered.

The larger lens was still held in a cracked shard of plastic, but that was no issue; in fact, it served as a handle.

"Yeah, let's see what we can do with this," said Alden. He grabbed a nearby piece of splintered wood, just a few inches long. Anything combustible would do. The sky was clear and the sun high—ideal conditions for a would-be pyromaniac with a microscope lens. He held the lens above the surface of the wood, adjusting up and down until the tiny dot of bright light focused there.

It only took a few seconds for some smoke to begin to form, and after a few more, a tiny flame erupted from the wood. Alden thrust his hands in the air.

"Woo-hoo! We did it, Burly! We have fire! We can cook things, and wash in hot water, and all kinds of stuff." Burly seemed unimpressed, but Alden let himself imagine that he recognized his tone of voice and was excited on the inside.

"Tell you what. Let's celebrate. Let's go get you some carrots and water, and then we'll set up a real campfire pit."

Alden climbed aboard his friend and they set off for the garden. Alden picked a few carrots to feed to an appreciative Burly, then picked a few more for his pouch. They went into the forest to the spring pond, then Alden rode while Burly wandered where he wished. He ambled some, but made his way to the fruitleaf bushes, where both Burly and Alden enjoyed a snack. Alden was fine with the fruitleaves fresh off the bush, but wondered how they would cook up, now that he was able to.

They spent a good part of the day in the deep forest, to some places Alden hadn't seen yet. That was always interesting. It felt good to have a touch of exploration to go with the survival activities of the day. As the afternoon was beginning to wane, Alden steered Burly back on the trek to the house. He did want to get some more done there so he could actually use a fire if he started one.

Alden figured the main thing he was going to do with a fire was hang his pot over it, and he had an idea for how to build something that would let him do that. He just wasn't sure if he had the muscle to get it done. At the base of the exterior house walls was a row of cement cinder blocks, and those were all still in place. If he could get those loose, he could arrange a circle on the ground, with a couple of stacks of blocks opposite each other. With a pipe or something set across the two stacks, he could hang the pot. If the holes of the cinder blocks were facing each other, he could even raise and lower the pipe.

When they got back to the house, Alden chose a block to work on. He got down on his knees in front of it, put both hands on the top edge, and gave a shove to try to tip it over.

No luck. He couldn't tell how the blocks were fastened to the ground, but whatever it was, it was stronger than Alden. He shoved again. Nothing.

With a little grunt, Burly strode up next to Alden and kicked a block. It caved in and smashed into a shell of cement pieces. But that gave Alden an idea.

"Good boy, Burly, good boy," he said. "Try it this way, though." Alden stepped over the row of blocks and turned around so he was facing Burly with the blocks between them. He got down and put his hand on a joint where two blocks met. Alden knew they were stronger there and might not break.

"Try it here, boy. Right here."

Burly did as Alden asked, and both blocks pulled up from the rock and tipped over, intact.

"Yes! Good boy. Here now." Alden put his hand on the joint between the next pair of blocks, and Burly kicked. Two more for the fire pit.

They went down the row—not without a couple of misses and crushed blocks—but before long Alden had twenty cinder blocks to build with. All around the base of the house, there were probably two hundred more. Those could be very valuable, even if he only managed to save half. For the time being, though, his twenty were enough to work with.

He was anxious to start on it, but he'd been around on his ankle enough, and carrying cinder blocks wasn't a great way to finish off the day. There was so much to do, and he needed to be able to move around easily. Alden got Burly to carry him back to his cave, and he rested for what he hoped would be a better ankle day coming up.

Chapter 13

In the morning, Alden was pleased to find his ankle was well enough to wear a shoe again. This was good. He had a lineup of living chores. Burly was in the forest, which made Alden feel better that he wouldn't be hanging around bored while Alden took care of business.

Back to the bridge stream to wash himself and his clothing. He had a decent collection of fresh clothes to change into, but rummaging around in the house debris had left both him and yesterday's outfit smudged with black char, to say nothing of his wrapped foot and the shirt bandage. He wanted a clean start.

Walking felt nearly normal. His ankle was weak, but not very painful. He took his kitchen pot with him on this trip, to get it rinsed and rubbed out and filled with water. He enjoyed his refreshing time in the stream. It was therapeutic. Like riding Burly, it made him feel close to the planet. He had several carrots with him from the day before, and he washed those up and ate two as he sat and let the stream rush around him. When he was finished, he donned his olive cargo shorts and blue T-shirt, with two socks and shoes, ready for the day.

As he ascended the ladder with pouch and pot, he decided water would best be fetched from the spring pond. It was strenuous and dangerous to try to get the pot up the ladder. Half-way up, he dumped some water out, but still had enough to make it worth the effort when he reached the top.

He'd been thinking about where to set up his fire pit, and decided it should be nearest his cave. Fire would likely be a late-day thing, and he didn't want to have to travel after he was finished with it for the night. Best, then, if he hauled his pot of water all the way back.

On the way, he stopped in the house debris field to check around for some type of piping to use as a crossbar over the fire. First, he went around the back to the realm of the appliances, to see if any kitchen plumbing was helpful. He stopped at the refrigerator to get a couple more of the water bottles out, and was hit with a nasty stench. Really old mayonnaise and cherry pie guts.

Alden realized it was a bad idea to leave the water in there for storage, and he removed all of the remaining bottles, an even dozen. They were slimy and disgusting. Alden lifted each one out by the lid with his fingertips and set it on the ground. It was too soon with his fresh water and clothes to devote something to wiping off the bottles. He'd just get them out of the decaying ooze in the frig and leave them for later washing. Maybe in hot water once he got a fire going.

He took a look around the debris from the south side

of the house, and there were a few pieces of broken tubes from the plumbing, but nothing very long. The bathroom might have had something, too. Something from the shower, maybe. That was on the other side of the house.

Alden walked through the foundation and house to where the bathroom had been. Perhaps because there was water there, or perhaps because the backup fuel drum that caused the worst of the burning had been on the south side, things from the bathroom were less charred and more just broken up. He saw a number of shattered shards of the shower stall. With some poking around, he discovered a chunk with plumbing attached. The shower head was sticking out of one side, and from the other was a short bit of plastic pipe, an elbow, and a six-foot length of pipe. This was perfect.

Alden used his hatchet to hack the long length from the elbow, and he flexed it a couple of times to test its strength. Plenty stiff enough to hold a pot of water. While he was looking for that, he located a couple other useful items: a pair of nail clippers and a toothbrush. That was a relief. His mouth was like fur, especially in the mornings. The toothbrush was something else he'd wash when he had hot water.

Alden put his new tools in his pouch, took the pot and his plumbing pipe, and headed off toward the cave. He didn't relish the thought of hauling twenty cinder blocks that same distance, and began thinking of how he could have Burly help with that. There was no question Burly would need to be dragging trees for the bridge, so it was time he rigged up some kind of pulling harness.

A harness meant rope; rope meant vines; vines meant a fresh tree down. It looked like the next thing on Alden's list was getting a tree chopped.

After a stop at the cave to drop things off and have a can of butter beans, Alden climbed out again and saw

Burly arriving.

"Hey, boy, great timing," Alden said. "Hate to run ya back to the forest right away, but we need to go get us a tree to work with. Let's do it."

Burly was obliging. On the ride, Alden began to ponder the enormity of what he was trying to undertake. He was going to try to chop down a two-foot tree with a five-inch hatchet blade. Then he was going to cut all the vines off it and tie and twist those into long lengths of construction rope. Then he was going to use some of the rope to make some kind of harness so Burly could drag the tree a thousand feet to the ravine. After that, he'd tip the tree into the ravine, in a position to be a leg post for the bridge, and tie it there somehow.

This was days of work. And when he was finished, he would need to do it a hundred times more. He would be at this for a year to get it done, and that's if nothing went wrong.

A year was an awfully long time for a boy of eleven to think about. He missed his parents from the pit of his soul, and this whole situation he was in was very, very unfair. No one had any good reason to do this to him. When he got away, and found out who it was, they'd be sorry.

Without even realizing it, Alden was crying. Burly was near the garden, and when Alden emitted a soft whimper or two, Burly stopped.

"Sorry, boy," Alden said with a broken voice. He slid down so he could talk to Burly in the eye.

"I don't mean to be weak, Burly. I'm sorry. I miss my mom and dad. I sure wish you could meet them. They would be totally amazed. It's hard for me to think about living here without them, and there's such a big, big job ahead of us." Alden rubbed Burly's snout.

"But don't worry, boy. Don't you ever think I'm going to give up on you and gettin' you home. I will never give up, Burly. Never." He paused, and his emotions welled up again. He sobbed some, then sniffled hard and got himself composed.

"Now let's go chop down a tree."

They were close enough to the edge of the forest that Alden decided to walk from there. In a few minutes, they were at the tree Alden hacked on earlier. He took the hatchet in both hands and took a stance.

"OK, here we go, Burly Boy."

Alden took a swing that landed. Not bad. He took another that didn't. Concentrate. More swings, more chips of moist wood. His ankle was more comfortable, and this was going better than before.

Chop. Chop. Drink of water. Chop. Dozens of chops. Carrot. Water. More chops. He was at it for an hour, and made a wedge in the tree about five inches deep. Burly was still hanging around.

"Holy cannoli. I need a real rest, boy," said Alden as he panted over to a fallen log and sat. He leaned forward with his elbows on his knees and took deep breaths. His arms and his back were sore. As soon as he could press on, though, he was up again.

"Now the other side. My dad cut one of these down with the chain saw so we could see the ring formation, and that's how he did it. Some on each side."

Alden started chopping away. He kept at it for most of another hour, pushing hard through progressively weakening fatigue and muscle pain. Although he was getting better and better at landing the hatchet where he wanted, he was only six inches into the opposite side of the tree. Between both wedges, about half the thickness of the trunk. He lifted one hand to the tree and gave the best shove he could muster. Nothing; it was still quite solid.

Alden was utterly spent. His arms were numb. He wondered how he was still gripping the hatchet, because his fingers seemed disconnected and out of his control. He couldn't stand straight; his posture was bent over forward, because his back was spastic and in deep pain. He couldn't even consider walking all the way over to his resting spot on the fallen log. He just dropped the hatchet and collapsed to the ground on his back.

Burly came over and put his head down, nostrils twitching with a couple of faint grunts.

"I'm OK, boy," Alden said with effort. "At least I'm gonna be. I'll have to keep that hatchet blade nice and sharp. No more swinging than I have to." He knew from Dad how to swipe a blade on a rock to keep the edge, and he made a mental note to add tool sharpening to the list of regular chores for the future.

Alden was intending to rest for just a few minutes and try to get back to it, but before he could consider that, he fell asleep.

When he awoke, Burly was lying on the ground next to him, to his right. On his left lay the tree.

"Whoa," said Alden. He raised his shoulders and rested on his elbows. "Burly, did you do this?"

Burly lifted his head, then rolled to his feet. Alden tried to get up as nimbly as he could, but he was very weak.

"Ouch, ouch, ouch," he said from one knee. "What did you do, boy?"

Burly stepped to the splintered trunk, lowered his head, and placed the top of it where the tree used to be.

"Wow, you did! You pushed the tree over. Well done, Burly. Good boy." Alden had managed to stand by that time, but not sturdily. His back was giving him fits. "This is terrific, boy. It'll help a lot if I don't have to chop all the way through."

Despite the nap, Alden had overdone it, and he was feeling a little bit nauseous. "Listen, boy, as much as I'd love to dig in here and start making ropes, I'm gonna have to hang it up for today. This took more out of me than I was thinkin'. I need to get some food and lie down."

Alden did love the idea of making rope. He really wished he was in better shape; now that the hard part was done, he could get going on something really useful and start their progress. Today, though, he would have to be satisfied with felling the tree. Tomorrow, there was much to be seen about how the vine ropes would work, and it excited him to find out.

Alden was astonished to learn just how sore he could be. Everything—legs, sides, back, arms—was in pain. Only his ankle was better, and even with that it was hard to tell, since everything else was way worse. He'd done plenty of outdoor work before, but never anything that concentrated and strenuous for that long. He was determined to work through it, though. Wearing himself out was no excuse for taking a day off when he had fresh vines to work with. True, he thought better of trying to fell another tree just yet. He could cut himself at least that much slack. But he needed to make progress, and there was a lot he could do even in his overexerted state.

When he climbed slowly out of his cave, Burly was nowhere to be seen. Feeling the way Alden did, this was no time to try to be an eager hiker. He took a deep breath, cupped his hands around his mouth, and yelled out for Burly. He knew better than to be too anxious or even assume Burly could hear him if he was deep in the woods, but after only a few seconds, he called again.

Thinking he might have to eventually walk the whole way, Alden started gingerly toward the forest. After fifty feet, he called out again to Burly, but as he was bringing his hands down he saw his enormous buddy trotting out of the foliage. Not a gallop this time, just a leisurely trot.

As Burly got closer, Alden smiled at watching everything in Burly's body jostle up and down with his bouncy steps, and Burly had a lot to jostle.

Burly slowed to a walk near the end, and Alden stepped carefully to meet him.

"Mornin', Burly Pal," he said with a rub of Burly's snout. "Time to cut us some vines today."

Alden was carrying his machete, thinking it would be a more applicable hacking tool for chopping the vines off a brushtop than his hatchet. The hatchet was still in his pouch, but there was a lot of deforestation coming up, and he was going to want whichever blade was best for the job.

Once Burly had rested a moment and Alden was atop his mammoth steed, he felt an urge to try something that was dangerous but suddenly seemed too thrilling not to experience. He wanted Burly to gallop.

"Hey, boy, let's try somethin' new," said Alden. "Let's make a charge to the forest. Let's run! Run, Burly Boy!" He gave Burly a couple strong nudges with his legs. "Are you with me? Let's do it." He nudged firmly again. Burly grunted.

"Oh, it'll be fine. I'll hang on. Come on!" Alden gave a good kick, and Burly took off. Alden suddenly clenched with his legs and held the vine reins tightly.

"Whoa-ho! That's it, boy!" Alden exclaimed, laughing. After a few awkward lurches while he got used to the movement, Alden could relax a bit and enjoy the ride. And what a rush it was. The thundering energy of Burly's rhythmic strides filled Alden with an indescribable exhilaration. Every image Alden could conjure of noble warriors atop waves of seismic burlons advancing triumphantly into history came vividly to life in his mind. Alden raised his machete in the air and let out a long, loud howl as Burly pounded across the open rock. It released something in Alden's soul and allowed him to immerse in a kind of freedom he hadn't felt in what seemed like forever.

Near the edge of the vegetation, Burly slowed, and Alden slid off him and hit the ground in stride before Burly even came to a stop. Burly was huffing the way he did, but was also nodding his head around with animation.

"I know, that's fun, huh," Alden said with a beaming smile. He couldn't suppress an excited giggle. Then he realized he was suppressing it, like he felt guilty for having a moment of emotional abandon. It sure was a strange life without parents. Feeling terrible was exactly that, but it also felt right. Feeling happy and free seemed like disrespecting his parents' memories. But it was bound to happen. It had to happen. It's what Mom and Dad would want for him. If there weren't going to be any people, they'd want him to have a friend like Burly.

"We should do that more," Alden said. He patted Burly's shoulder. "Let's get you a treat."

They stopped at the garden for a carrot for Burly. Alden gave a quick look up and down the rows and made note that it was going to be time for weeding before long. Also, the green beans were about to come in. He was all right with green beans, but knew he wouldn't be fond of eating those raw, and that meant getting his fire pit ready. So much to do.

The vines from the fallen brushtop were roughly twenty feet long. Alden grabbed a bundle in his hand near the top of the tree—eight vines—and hacked them free. Right at the top, where the vines met the tree trunk, each vine was quite stout; more than an inch in diameter. They tapered quickly, though, to a manageable and more flexible thickness. He took his fresh vines to find a place to sit, and started working with them to make a rope. They were nice and pliable, just as Alden had planned.

At first, he took five and just twisted them in a spiral for about five feet. He flexed it around and pulled on it, and it was certainly plenty strong, but it didn't stay together well. Then he kept four of them straight and spiraled the fifth around those. That was a little better, so Alden tried to work with it some, wrapping it around a tree and tying knots. It was bulky. As soon as the vines weren't completely fresh, and began to stiffen, it was going to get too difficult in a hurry.

He kept Burly up to date with running commentary the whole time. He also used Burly to test the strength of his new rope, tying a loop for him to pull on against a standing tree. Through all that, though, Alden decided five vines were just too many to try to deal with for as long and as many wraps and knots as this whole project was going to take.

Alden started over with three vines, and he had an idea from how his mother used to wear her hair. She often had it in a woven pattern she called a braid, but Alden didn't know how she did it. If he could figure it out, it would keep the vines tight to each other, like a real rope. He went through a few attempts with intricate windings that didn't work, then realized he was probably making it harder than it needed to be. He began again with a simpler weave, just laying one on top of another, and pretty soon, Alden figured out how to braid. It was perfect.

"Hey, this is it," he said. "Burly, I know how to make rope. We're in business!"

He made loops and tied knots and checked the strength. It passed the Burly test. He knew he would need lengths longer than twenty feet, so he knotted ends together and kept braiding. Alden wasn't trying to use the very thickest part of the vines near the treetop, but they were nevertheless noticeably tapered from the top end to the bottom, so he also swapped ends on some so his three vines were a combination of thin spots and thick spots. That would keep the strength uniform and make sure he didn't end up with a very thick end to work with after the vines dried some and stiffened. Alden hoped he could work it out so he was always tying fresh vines, letting them cure in place in the bridge frame, but it was too early to know how successful that would be.

For the moment, he was just happy he could proceed with rope production, hoping life held more successes in the days ahead.

Chapter 14

Alden's afternoon was fruitful. Once he had about sixty feet of braided vine rope, he went to Burly to fashion a pulling harness. First, he draped the rope over his own head, leaned forward, and pantomimed dragging something heavy. By this time, he had no reason to suspect Burly wouldn't realize what he was doing; he'd caught on to everything else.

Then, as he spoke to Burly continuously about how great this was going to be and how they needed to get lots of trees over to the bridge, he draped the middle of the rope over Burly's collar. He chose one of the rounded points on each side of the plate, low near Burly's knees to keep the pulling force in line with his body, and looped the rope around it once. That gave him the two ends trailing behind, ready to tie to something draggable.

Alden had cut all the vines from the tree, so the top of it was just a mass of stubby vine stalks. He brought Burly over near the tree and got the ropes around it a couple of times, but when he led Burly forward to test the harness it slipped off the tree. Alden figured that was par for the course, as it seemed nothing he ever tried worked the first time through. Far from being daunted by that, though, Alden always saw it as a lesson that needed learning—just one way not to do it. Then two ways, then as many ways as it took until the way that worked.

He learned that attitude from his parents. Dad, mostly. As a pioneer, problems would often seem huge, and would often require innovation to solve. Innovation took perseverance. Huge problems could always be solved by just figuring out the next step. Stay focused through enough steps, and the problems are tackled. As deeply as he missed his parents, Alden was in tune with the understanding that one of the best ways to honor them was to persevere and get this done. Do it for yourself, for Mom and Dad, and for Burly. The rope slipping off the tree was a small thing in the grand scheme, but these were the kinds of moments that kept him reinforcing his resolve.

The brushtops naturally tapered from bottom to top. A forty-foot tree that was two feet wide at the bottom was only a foot wide up where all the vines came out. That meant looping the rope near the bottom instead of the top would pull against the wider trunk and prevent it from slipping off.

So, on his second try, Alden had a method that worked. Now it was time to see if Burly could pull the weight.

Alden stood at Burly's head and patted his snout. "Are you ready to try this, boy?"

Without hesitation, Burly tossed his head a little,

seemingly in defiance of the possible difficulty of the task, and took off.

"Whoa! All right, boy," said Alden as he twisted out of the way and took a couple quick steps to right himself and catch up. Burly was clearly working at it, but his pace was smooth. He was walking nearly as quickly as he did without the load.

"Wow. That's the way, Burly Boy," Alden said with a big smile. There was no end to the amazing feats of this astonishing companion. Amid the simple wonder at the display of power, Alden was also greatly pleased that this critical aspect of the bridge construction would plainly not be an issue. Many trees would need to be hauled to the bridge. Lots of them could be lighter than this one, too, because Alden could let them dry out in the woods first. Without all that stored water in the trunk, the load would lessen, and that made Alden happy, too.

Although Alden was prepared to guide Burly around the end of the garden—the one opposite the water pipe— he never really needed to. Burly knew exactly what he was doing, something that was becoming less and less of a surprise to Alden. More awe, less surprise.

Burly made it to the bridge without stopping, and although he didn't seem entirely spent, he was huffing and a little fidgety, like after galloping. Despite still feeling terrific soreness from the previous day's tree chopping, Alden walked the whole way. He knew he'd want to be able to ride Burly on these trips, but thought better of burdening him with that on this first run. Maybe when the load was a dry tree.

At the bridge came the next big challenge: standing the tree in the ravine. It seemed the straightforward approach was to get it pushed off the edge of the existing bridge piece, but the question there was whether or not Burly could push as effectively as he pulled. Burly needed a rest, though, and Alden took a few minutes to have some water and stand at the ravine, thinking about how all this needed to work.

It was hard not to be in a hurry, but Alden mustered his patience and did his best to figure it out the right way. He took off his pouch, set it down nearby, and got to work. First, he had Burly haul the tree just as close to the edge of the bridge as he could. That kept the base of the tree toward the bridge, which was the right direction. When it tipped, he wanted the base down in the ravine. Then, he untied the vine rope and guided Burly to the other end of the tree, reattaching the rope and having Burly pull sideways a little to line it up straight.

Next was the big moment. Alden used his usual pantomime instructions for Burly, getting down on all fours and placing his head on the top of the tree. Also as usual, Burly understood immediately. He got in place and lowered his head. As if figuring out a problem himself, Burly first noticed that he couldn't get the top of his head onto the tree trunk without hitting his snout on the ground if he went straight down. He grunted and twisted his head, setting it askew. That worked.

Burly began pushing. This was obviously more difficult than dragging, but Burly used more and more effort until the tree began to slide.

"Yes, that's it! You are amazing!" said Alden as he was standing on the bridge, ready to grab or guide or something—he wasn't sure yet—when the tree tipped into the ravine. Burly kept at it as the base of the tree extended out over the edge. Alden could see that it got a little easier at that point, with less and less weight on the ground, and Burly sped up. Alden threw up his hands and ran to him.

"Stop! Stop!" Burly couldn't see him, but when Alden put his hands on the back of his turned head, he quit pushing. The tree was very close to the tipping point, but still resting on the ground.

"Slow now, boy," said Alden as he did his best to mimic slow pushing. He held his hands out in front of him with a small gap between them. "Not very far to go now."

Burly put his head down on the tree and gave a shove, nudging it about a foot.

"Great! Great, Burly. Hold it right there," Alden said, gesturing a two-handed stop sign with his palms forward.

Alden went quickly back to the edge of the bridge. "I'm going to try something here." He got on his knees next to the tree, reached out, and pushed down on the part hanging in the air. The tree tipped a little.

"Cool. We're really close," he said.

He pushed down harder on the tree, and the top rose promisingly, but came back down. With one more good shove, Alden got it to tip high enough to go over. The tree came close to vertical as it slid quickly down the edge and Alden bolted to his feet to react to whatever he saw happening.

It landed with a thud. The top of the tree stuck four feet above the bridge level, which was perfect, and it was near enough to Alden for him to touch. It didn't have enough lean on the bridge deck to stay in place, though, and began to tip to the right.

Alden instinctively took a step that direction, his toes at the edge, and reached out with his right hand to grab the tree. He could immediately tell one hand was not going to accomplish anything, and he instinctively reached around the brushtop with both arms. Even so, Alden had no real leverage to change its course.

The tree went down, and Alden went with it.

Alden screamed as he fell. The direction of the toppling tree took Alden's trajectory upstream a little in the ravine, and that saved his life. Alden unintentionally did most of a somersault in the air and landed on his back in the thick brush, to the sound of the tree crashing into bushes just next to him.

The echoes of the ravine died down. Alden was quiet, looking at the deep blue sky and assessing what had just happened. He took a quick mental survey of his body, and nothing was complaining too much. Not alarmingly so, anyway. He had some surface pain in his legs. Probably some scratches, maybe some bleeding. Something was poking him in the back, but more on the order of discomfort than injury. His arms were good.

He slowly rolled to his left, toward the fallen tree, to see more of where he was. When he did, his right arm was resting on the tree trunk, near the top, and his head was facing down. At the bare ground. He had landed in the very first row of bushes that were not cleared by the Sec Crew when the bridge was built.

"Holy cannoli," said Alden under his breath.

A sound came from above. It was a low moan, the kind only one creature Alden knew could make. He craned his head around to look and see Burly up at the edge of the ravine.

"I'm OK, boy," said Alden. "That was close." Burly blurted a brief snort of acknowledgement.

With minor difficulty, Alden pulled himself out of the bushes and rolled onto the ground. He looked at his legs; as he expected, some scrapes, but nothing deep. He stood, brushing and straightening his clothes. Good thing he took off his pouch—the hatchet could have caused some serious problems in a fall like that. His safari hat was a few feet away, none the worse for wear. He retrieved it and started toward the ravine ladder.

"Guess I need to figure something out," Alden said in a way that was indirectly at Burly, who was too far away to really hear him. It was more just thinking out loud. He was starting up the ladder as he added, "Gotta have a way to keep the trees where I need 'em when they go in the ravine."

Despite the incident, Alden was also thinking about what went right. They got the tree to the ravine. They got it in place and pushed over really well. The tree height was ideal. He just had to keep it standing where he needed it.

When he reached the top, Burly was there. Alden gave him a pat. "Thanks for checking on me, boy."

Alden paused and considered what to do next. The sun was low, and he was feeling like he'd had enough excitement for the day. Burly had worked hard and given him everything he could have asked for. He decided to get back to his cave, but there was one more thing to accomplish as they did.

He had Burly stop at the house foundation on their way past. Alden figured if Burly could drag a tree around, twenty cinder blocks were no sweat. He was right.

He strung all the loose cinder blocks for the fire pit on the harness rope and tied the loop closed. Burly effortlessly hauled them the rest of the way to the cave, where Alden picked a spot and arranged a dozen of them in a circle. The other eight he stacked in two columns of four each, opposite each other across the circle. He retrieved his plumbing pipe and set it over the top. A nice fit, and plenty strong.

"There we go, Burly," said Alden. "Now we can have us a fire. Not today. Not enough sun left, and we've done enough for today." He stepped over to Burly. Instead of his usual pat on the snout, he went near his collar and put his arms around the back of Burly's head, resting his face on the top of it.

"Thank you, boy. Thank you for helping, and caring, and being my friend, and giving me a reason to stay alive. I love you, Burly."

He stood upright again, and took the harness rope off of Burly's neck plate. "Now go get some rest. Tomorrow'll have plenty more work waiting for us."

Chapter 15

I remember a lot of feelings from that life. I remember intense grief. I recall heartbreak. And excitement, and deep friendship, and even affection, in a fashion. Pride. Anger. Real wonder. And terror. True, heart-stopping terror.

It was a moment. Just a moment. But one so far removed from anything I feel now, it stands alone. The vision in my head is so clear. It's like a photo I can pull up and examine in detail whenever I want. At the same time, it's a photo someone else took. They took it and showed me, and I can never forget it. Young Alden took that photo.

Alden rose from his cave ready to dive into another sunny, gorgeous day on Cappa Terse. He had some ideas on how to deal with the tree situation in the ravine, but there were also other things demanding attention.

Washing, the garden, collecting firewood. In his pouch was the hatchet, water, and a change of clothes. Alden was primed for whatever the day needed to be.

Burly was away in the forest, and rather than trek to the ravine stream right away, Alden started off for the woods, to meet Burly and pull some carrots before his washing session. His ankle was in pretty good shape now; it only felt slightly different from his uninjured foot, and he didn't think about it much at all.

He'd made it across two hundred of the thousand feet between his cave and the garden area when he saw Burly lumbering out of the vegetation toward him. Perfect timing again. It wouldn't surprise Alden to learn Burly had some kind of sense of when Alden was up and around.

Alden glanced around the sky and noticed something else. The enormous bird was circling again. It was just to his left and moving counterclockwise, so it continued in an arc farther to his left. Alden kept walking, but as the bird circled more behind him, he stopped to watch. He didn't say anything. He was fascinated by why this huge bird would be coming out to the plateau. There were no crawling animals there. It was awesome to watch, but it didn't make sense.

After a few more moments, Alden had his answer. The winged predator dropped lower in the sky and made a tight turn in its flight path. It was now headed straight in Alden's direction.

Instantly, Alden knew what was happening. Horrified that he was the prey the bird was scouting on the plateau, he turned to run, and saw that Burly was already galloping toward him.

"Burly!" Alden yelled as he dropped the pouch on the run as deftly as he could. "*Burly!*"

Alden was already so frightened he thought he might pass out, and he struggled to keep his feet under him.

His heart was racing. His breath panting far beyond the exertion. He'd never been this scared. Not in his entire life.

The whole thing took scant seconds. The gap between Alden and Burly was closing, but Alden didn't know how long he had. He only looked over his shoulder once to see where the bird was. When he did, what he saw struck to his core.

The bird was only ten feet behind him. It's wingspan was almost twice that, so it blotted out the sky. It was mostly black, but it's chest was red. A deep, threatening, blood red. And the weapons. It had a beak with a curve and a point on the end that looked like he could rip rocks in two. Its talons were flared, ready to grab, each one a scythe at least a foot long, on gnarled, grey-yellow feet.

Most disturbing of all were its eyes. It had piercingly intense black eyes beneath feathered ridges of eyebrow, with a maniacal look of focused evil. It was more than survival. This creature would take immense pleasure in impaling Alden on its razored claws and crushing his head with a single bite.

Alden was too petrified to keep running, and he fell to the ground as the bird reached for him. Reached, but could not quite grab. In a full gallop, Burly had put his head down to throw his bony plate forward as far as it could go, and he gave a thundering lunge into the air. He only left the ground a few inches, but it was enough to strike the bird squarely at the top of its chest. Alden heard the blunt thud of the impact and a loud crack of the bird's neck. Burly landed on his feet and pulled up, as if this type of acrobatics was all in a day's work, as the bird flopped and rolled and came to a motionless stop.

"Burly!" said Alden, deeply terror-stricken. "Burly, are you OK?"

Burly looked at Alden, but was trotting over to the

bird. He nudged at it a couple of times with his snout. No movement. Burly then turned and trotted toward Alden, who was getting to his feet. Burly was huffing mightily from the exertion.

"Burly, are you OK, boy?" said Alden urgently. He wanted to give Burly another big hug, but knew better until Burly had his breath back. Burly just stood and panted.

"You saved my life, Burly Boy. Holy cannoli, you were amazing! You jumped right up and nailed that thing. That was the most incredible thing I've ever seen!"

Burly tossed his snout toward Alden's arm and gave a quick grunt. Alden had scarcely noticed yet, but there was blood running down his right arm and a sharp pain above his elbow. The bird's reach had gotten so close that one laser-pointed talon tore an eight-inch gash in Alden's upper arm. Six inches of his shirt sleeve were sliced, too. Now that Alden was paying attention to the new laceration, the feel of it became acute.

"Wow, I guess he got me, huh, boy," said Alden, holding his arm and examining the wound. "Wow, this hurts."

Alden moved toward his pouch, back where he dropped it while he was running. "I'd better get this bandaged up right away."

He took the fresh T-shirt from his pouch and did his best to get it wrapped and tied around his arm, using his teeth to hold one end of the knot. It stung quite a bit. Once he had that, he was intensely curious about the bird, and walked over to give it a good look.

It was simply huge. Its body was six feet long, not counting the tail. The wings were mangled from the crash landing, and its fearsome talons were curled up to its lifeless feet. Alden gave it a little kick in the side.

"Not so tough now, huh," said Alden. "Not when you try and mess with Burly."

Burly had ambled over and was now standing next to Alden. Now was the time for a hug, and Alden put his arms around the back of Burly's head.

"Thanks, boy."

Alden studied and thought about the bird for a moment.

"Whatcha think, Burly? Should I try to figure out how to cook him? We can make fire now." Alden was intrigued by the idea, and presumed this was the only chance he'd ever have to eat freshly cooked meat, but hadn't the first notion of how to go about it. Eventually, he decided against.

"Well, I think it's not worth it, old pal. I have no idea how to do that, and if I can't get it done right now, it'll rot. Then it'd be poison. Better let it go."

Alden was thinking more about the rot, and realized that either way, he had to move the carcass.

"Can't let it sit here, though. Tell you what. We'll get some carrots, then drag this guy down to the ravine, down past the bridge, where he won't bother us. One thing, though."

Alden reached down and grabbed one of the talons. It was so massive his hand barely clasped all the way around the base of it. The tip had blood on it.

"I'm keepin' this one," he said. He took out the hatchet and took a couple hacks at the toe. It was little awkward, as he had to swing with his left hand; his right arm was hurting too much to use it that way. Eventually, the talon came free. "This one's a souvenir." Alden put the talon in his pouch, and they headed off for the garden.

Alden could have ridden Burly on the way there, but he wanted to walk off the anxious energy. He was a bundle of nerves. He couldn't help but scan the sky every few seconds, but there were no more birds. Was that the same one circling earlier? Was that the only one that knew he was there? He had no way of knowing.

Seeing the dead bird on the ground was reassuring as far as the existing danger was concerned, but it didn't reduce the primal fear of that moment when he saw the thing ready to rip him to shreds. It was so close. That was part of the shock. He didn't know what to expect, but was alarmed that the bird had zoomed in so fast. Looking behind him and seeing the bird practically on top of him was a zing of adrenaline unlike anything Alden had been through before.

They got to the garden and Alden pulled some carrots, feeding several to Burly right away. Alden had left the hoe with the broken handle nearby, and he took the time to walk the rows and dig up the larger weeds.

The chores consumed a good chunk of the morning. From the garden, Alden wanted to go all the way back to his cave to get a fresh bandage. His T-shirt was well-soaked with blood. There, Alden draped Burly's rope harness back on, and they went back to the dead bird to haul it to the ravine. Alden led them well past the bridge and shoved the carcass over the edge where he didn't think the rotting would have a chance to bother them or the water supply.

Next, it was back to the bridge for Alden to get some washing done. His clothes, his body, his arm. Some carrots, too. He had brought the shirt he used to wrap his ankle, as that was better suited as a bandage than a T-shirt, but it was quite dirty from all the walking. He scrubbed everything up as best he could, then let the stream wash over the wound for a while. It stung at first, but soothed, and he gingerly ran a fingertip through the gash a couple times to rub out dirt that may have gotten ground in when he fell. It was painful, but he never hesitated; this was part of his survival, and it was easier to face things like injuries than the emotions of his situation. He got the shirt bandage wrapped and tied securely and went on about his business.

With his arm in that condition, his business was going to be braiding vines. He'd used fewer than twenty to make the rope harness he had, and there were roughly a hundred more from that first tree, so he had plenty to keep him busy. Toss in a trip to the fruitleaf bushes, and an attempt to make a fire while the sun was still high enough, and the day would fill up quickly.

It went without incident, but the afternoon did fly by, and Alden was left needing to hurry to collect burnables for the fire pit. Things from the forest floor, mostly: dry leaves and vine bits, plus thicker twigs and branches from the stouter bushes. For logs, he planned on using chunks of wood from the house frame that had splintered and scattered around. It wasn't difficult to find some of those.

With Burly observing, Alden built a small teepee of twigs over a pile of leaves in the center of his ring of cinder blocks. It was beginning to get late, but Alden made it in time to use the available sun. With his microscope eyepiece lens, the leaves ignited on cue, and from burning twigs, Alden was able to construct a roaring collection of house boards.

The pot he'd filled with water two days earlier was still sitting near the cave, and Alden wasn't sure he'd want to drink out of it, but could certainly use it to see how his cooking setup would work. He strung the shower plumbing pipe through the pot handle and hoisted it up to the top of the stacks of blocks. The pipe bowed, but held well. It was too high for the water to be much affected by the flames, but that was good. It meant he would have great adjustability for keeping something slightly warm.

Through constant comments to Burly about the relative success of this endeavor and the benefits of fire, Alden lowered the pipe by a few holes, until the flames were nicely surrounding the pot. It looked great. Alden sat on the ground just outside the pit and watched the flames, waiting to see how long it would take for the water to boil. In a rare move, Burly flopped his mammoth frame down not far from Alden, with his head facing the fire.

"Hey, there you go, boy," said Alden. "Time to relax. The fire's pretty, isn't it?" It occurred to Alden that Burly had likely not seen a lot of fire, but he wasn't at all disturbed by it. On the contrary, Burly seemed instantly soothed. It made Alden smile to think they would be able to share and appreciate campfires together.

The anticipation of boiling water proved to be less than satisfied. Within a couple of minutes, the heat was too much for the plastic plumbing rod. It began to bow, then quickly buckled in two. The pot landed in the fire and tipped over, dousing it almost completely.

"Aw, man," said Alden, rising to his feet. Burly also rolled himself up. "Look at this, Burly." He put a knee on the ring of blocks and reached in to the pot handle. It wasn't hot yet, and he lifted it out. There was a faint smell of burned plastic.

"Pew. Well, we were close, boy. Should've known better than that, huh. I'll have to find something else." He set the pot down and retrieved the pieces of pipe from the pit. "Not tonight, though. I'll see what I can find tomorrow. Guess we should hang it up for now. Go on and do what ya do. I'll see you in the mornin'."

Alden went to the cave for the night, partly disappointed but partly satisfied. He'd get it figured out, and when he did, they could have evenings at a campfire. That made him smile as he drifted off, and smiling his way to sleep was precious.

Chapter 16

hen morning came, Burly was waiting for Alden outside the cave.

"Mornin', Burly Boy," said Alden. "Anxious to get to it today? All right, let's have at it."

Alden climbed on board and guided Burly toward the bridge. The shirt bandage on his right arm was the best one for the job, but he wanted to clean it again. His arm was hurting more today. Besides that, he figured the cross beam for the fire pit needed to be metal, and the only place he knew where there was metal was in the ravine. He might be able to find a piece that could work. On the way there, Alden couldn't help but glance around at the skies in case another of those birds came around, but there was only the blue and a few wispy clouds.

In the ravine, Alden washed everything again. Clothes, body, bandage. He took his time and scrubbed as best he could manage. With the bandage off, he examined his arm wound, and the surrounding skin was beginning to redden. Alden figured that was part of the trauma from the ripping talon, and he wrapped it up again and got dressed.

Searching for metal was an adventure, because so . much of the bridge frame fell into the bushes, and many pieces of the wreckage were way too thick for him to handle. With some work, though, he was able to locate a few sections of smaller angle iron bracing. One was longer than he needed, but bent in a good place. If he could get it broken off where the bend was, it might do the job.

Alden was just able to get it up the ladder with him, and he went to work figuring out how to bend the angled bar. He found a rock he could lean it on, and he had a handy burlon who could step on it. Then he turned it over and got it bent the other direction, then again, and again. Eventually it got weak and broke.

"Now, we're in business, Burly," said Alden, leaning the bar on his neck collar while he mounted. He hoisted the bar across his lap. "Back to the fire pit, boy."

The angle iron was a teeny bit shorter than the plumbing pipe, but still long enough to rest on both stacks of cinder blocks, and that was all he needed.

"Look at that, boy," Alden said with a smile. "We're back in the cooking business. If we get some time later, we'll go fill up the pot. For now, though, I wanna get to the forest and make some more rope."

They stopped at the garden again, and Alden took inventory of the carrots. Only a couple dozen left. It would be time to move on to green beans soon, once they matured.

Alden still had lots of vines available to braid, but he didn't want to wait long to get another tree cut down, either. Hatchet in hand, he chose a nearby brushtop, took a deep breath, and began chopping. He could tell he was a little better at it than when he started the first one, but only an inch into the tree he had to stop. His right arm was hurting too much, and it was making him feel weak.

He moved on, braiding rope. That was better, but even so, after half an hour he was dog tired. This wasn't normal.

Alden thought maybe he needed a snack, but he didn't have any clean carrots with him, and he thought a rest on Burly's back might do some good, so they headed out to the fruitleaf bushes. They ate, and Alden picked some leaves for his pouch. When they returned, Alden braided some more rope, but weaving every strand was effort. He didn't feel sick; he just never had any energy. Maybe he was just overdoing things, but he was getting lots of sleep and never had this problem before. It didn't make sense.

Before he pooped out completely, Alden stopped his work and got Burly to take him to the fire pit. His empty pot was there, and he wanted to have it full of water. It was going to take some time to do all the traveling to the pit, to the ravine stream, and back, and he thought he should get started on that.

Hoisting the pot of water up the ladder was extremely difficult. He couldn't carry the water in his right hand. That hurt too much. But that meant holding the ladder rungs with it as he ascended all the way, and that was no picnic, either. It was hurting him a lot. More of a dull, throbbing pain than the stinging he experienced before.

It took considerable concentration, but he got to the bridge surface without falling or dropping the pot. Once there, though, he faced the long trek over to the fire pit. There was no good way to travel on Burly with a pot of water, so he was left with hauling it the whole way himself. He stopped twice to rest, and when he finally made it to the pit, he had nothing left. There was no way he had the stamina to start another fire. Spent, he said goodnight to Burly and settled into his cave to collapse into slumber.

❮❖❯

Alden awoke to the sound of Burly crying out with a moan. He noticed right away from the angle of sun through the cave hole that it was higher than it ever was when he got up.

"I'm OK, Burly," Alden said right away to calm his friend. "I'll be right up."

His arm was hurting a lot. He hadn't done anything with his bandage overnight—and hadn't planned to—but now he was wondering if he should be changing it more often. The arm felt strange to move, besides the pain. It felt puffy. When he sat up and reached to untie the shirt bandage, Alden could see that below and above it was some swelling.

He removed the shirt and was a little disturbed by the look of the gash. It was redder; the redness went almost halfway around his arm from the cut. The wound itself was a little bit open, and while not really bleeding, was seeping in spots. It was far longer than any cut he'd seen, and that made him slightly uncertain of what was normal for this kind of wound, but he was pretty sure it was infected. He just didn't know what to do about that. He had no medications, topical or internal, so his plan for the moment was to hope his body knew how to fight it off.

Standing was oddly difficult. In fact, Alden didn't even make it to his feet on the first try. He got part way up and had to sit down again. It wasn't from dizziness; it just took more effort than he was expecting. It was like shoving with his legs just to get upright.

Climbing wouldn't be normal, either. On the first

reach with his right hand, a new bolt of pain shot through him, and he dropped it to his side. With some effort, he was able to get to the top, but it was tiring. Burly was standing very near the cave opening.

"Hey, boy," said Alden. "Sorry I slept so long."

Burly raised his snout a little and waved it toward Alden's injured arm.

"Yeah, kind of nasty lookin', isn't it. I'm not going to be much use today, buddy." Alden walked a few steps to the fire pit ring and sat on a cinder block.

"I don't know what to tell you, boy. I'm not good for much. I think I'm just gonna get something to eat and rest today." He stood up again and patted Burly's snout. "I'm OK. I'll be right as rain in a little while. You just have a day to yourself and I'll be better real soon."

Alden made his way back to the cave hole and lowered himself slowly inside. He had two cans of food, trying to keep his strength up; one was salmon, one was yellow wax beans. The beans were not his favorites, but he ate those first, knowing he'd have salmon to satisfy his palate. Since he wasn't going to be doing anything outside, he left his wound unbandaged and laid back on his sleeping log. He'd never had much success trying to sleep during the day, even when he was sick, but he nodded off in only a few minutes.

The sun angle was well into the afternoon when Alden awoke, and he didn't feel well at all. The arm was throbbing, red, and swollen, and Alden was weak and slightly nauseous. He didn't try to get up, thinking more sleep would be the best thing for him, and luckily it didn't take long before he was out again.

Several times through the evening and night the same scene played out, with Alden hoping beyond hope that the morning sun would somehow be a magic wand that would show him improvement.

No such magic was at hand, as morning arrived and

Alden was even worse. Suffering through chills and sweat now, he knew he was feverish and the infection was worsening. Maybe spreading. He'd heard of that happening when things like this got really bad. He'd also heard of slicing and draining infected wounds—Dad had to have that done once—but the thought of that made him even more nauseous. Every time he'd ever been sick, the mantra was to drink fluids, so he forced himself to sit up and have as much of a bottle of water as he could get down. He knew of nothing else but fluids and rest, so he lay back down to see if he could sleep.

Sleep he did, but fitfully. Cold and hot and sweating either way, he was starting to have periods when he couldn't tell if he was asleep or not, if dreams were real. It was frightening, because his hazy mind was creating awful visions of both he and Burly stricken with deadly illness, or drowning in his cave full of water, or any of a number of disastrous predicaments. He rose to lucidness just long enough to reassure himself that the last terror was an illusion, then he sank back into delirious fear.

Alden regained consciousness and swam through the mental fog into a moment of relative clarity. In that moment, he knew immediately that something had to be done. The swelling was in his chest now, and all the way down his arm, and the wound itself was large and tight with disgusting fluid.

He was in no condition to do anything, beginning with simply standing up, but he had to. He was dead if he didn't. He was going to have to open up the wound and drain it.

The only thing he knew of that could do that job was his machete, and that was still in the woods where he'd been using it to hack tree vines. There was one other thing sharp enough to get it done—the bird talon—but there was every chance the talon had some kind of poison or something else about it that caused this in the first place. That was too much of a risk.

He was going to have to go get the machete. What's more, he was going to have to sterilize it. Alden knew that much about germs, at least. Boiling things sterilizes them. There was log-sized wood in the fire pit from the pot-tipping incident, and that was probably dry again by now, but no twigs or leaves. A trip to the forest would need to include fetching kindling along with the machete.

A trip to the forest. It was exhausting to even think it.

Alden moved very slowly toward standing. His breathing was short. His arm felt as if the bird had succeeded in ripping it entirely away. He never actually made it all the way to his feet. He rolled off the log to his knees and scooted on those over to the ladder, grabbing his pouch, the microscope eyepiece lens, and his shirt bandage along the way.

With a left-hand grasp of a rung, he heaved up and got one leg almost under him, then another heave allowed him the other. Breathing heavily, the ladder was a tremendous challenge, as he didn't trust his grip alone to keep him on the ladder in his state. He had to hook his left arm through each rung to the elbow, rest, then get his feet on the next rung and shove. Then rest. Then quickly move his left hand to the next rung, secure it to the elbow, and repeat.

At the top, Burly was very close nearby, moaning lightly.

"I've got trouble, boy," said Alden before he was even all the way out of the cave opening. He paused before he kept speaking, but it was only because his thoughts didn't collect into words cohesively enough to go any faster. "I don't know how we're gonna do this, but I've got to get to the forest and collect some fire kindling and my machete."

Alden still didn't stand on his way to Burly. He couldn't maintain strength or balance well enough for that. He crawled to Burly's side and took hold of the vine stirrup still hanging where he'd put it, and, like the stairs, pulled and got himself upright, though leaning on Burly. He put a foot in the stirrup and took several breaths to work up the energy to have a go at mounting, and he almost made himself pass out in the process. After he got prepared as best he could expect, he mustered up everything and made a heroic vault onto Burly's back.

"OK, boy," Alden said, panting and grimacing in pain. "To the forest."

Alden never thought twice about how long a walk it was from the cave to the nearest portions of the forest. He made reasonable efforts to consolidate trips or plan chores according to travel time, but the walking was part of life, and he couldn't afford to consider a jaunt from the cave to the forest or bridge any differently from going between the living room and kitchen. Not on a regular daily basis.

Today was anything but regular. Farthest from. And today the trip was interminable. Burly hadn't taken more than three steps before Alden thought he was going to fall off, lie on the ground, and die from his infection. It was impossible to focus his mind, drifting in and out of perceiving anything around him. He had no reliable way to help himself think straight, so when he could sense that his delirium was getting especially dangerous, he gave himself a pat on the right arm. The bolt of pain brought him out of the fog, at least for a few minutes.

Burly was doing his best; Alden could feel that Burly was moving quickly and yet more smoothly and carefully under him, somehow understanding in his amazing way that this was urgent but Alden was fragile.

Alden had struggled through three-quarters of the way when his balance completely escaped him, and he waivered and drifted, then toppled off to his right. On the way down, the thought went through Alden's mind that this was the end, and he closed his eyes as if that would somehow shut it all out. The agony when he crashed into the rock surface was something beyond his youthful imagining.

He lay in the suddenly oppressive sun wondering why he still had to be alive, every heart beat pounding searing pain through his upper body. He thought back to the first moments after his parents were murdered, and how he had not thrown himself into the ravine. This was what he feared—not instant relief, but wallowing in torturous anguish, waiting through an eternity of torment to slip into merciful death. Alden pondered the irony that in spite of everything he'd tried to do, it still came to this moment, this desperate longing to once and for all rid that forsaken planet of the last, forgotten vestige of humanity.

Chapter 17

Slowly writhing in speechless delirium, Alden became aware of a scraping sensation on his left arm. The first time was dismissed as hallucination, but the second and third demanded attention.

Alden opened his eyes and saw Burly at his side, licking him, his rough, wet tongue beckoning for revival. Burly. Why did Burly have to be there? Alden's mind was awash in conflict, loving Burly for his compassion and cursing him for being the ever-present reason to push on. If Alden passed away, Burly was condemned to the plateau. He was Alden's responsibility.

In his next moments, Alden was cursing himself, too, for languishing in his indulgent desires to abandon his friend and leave everything behind. There would be no such luxury. Not on this day. He swallowed what spit he could gather and spoke.

"OK, boy," he said in a withered voice. "I promised to get you home. I know I did. I'll fix this. Don't you worry."

Alden rolled to his left to raise up on his elbow, focusing his resolve on blocking the pain from his mind and renewing his determination. Keeping his right arm at his side, he got to his knees. He motioned in a circle with his left hand, in a way Burly knew meant to turn so the vine stirrup was in front of Alden.

"Let's do this."

Again, Alden pulled on the stirrup, got to his feet, and wearily vaulted himself onto Burly's back. Burly turned and headed once more for the forest.

Alden tried to help himself concentrate better by talking to Burly, even telling him that if he stopped talking, Burly should call out and snap him out of it. That might have been more than Burly could understand, but by this time Alden knew better than make any assumptions about what Burly could or could not comprehend.

The strategy did seem to work. By forcing himself to speak, Alden reduced the tendency to drift away in his thoughts. Even if all he said was how much pain he was in, forming the words kept his attention on maintaining concentration. It also helped the time pass, and soon they were where they needed to be. Alden struggled but managed the coherency to guide Burly near his machete before attempting to dismount.

Alden slipped off of Burly, with sufficient control to both land and stay on his feet long enough to lower himself gently to his knees without toppling straight to the ground. In only a few moments, Alden scraped up twigs and leaves, put them in his pouch, and picked up his machete. Still conscious of the danger of slicing the pouch with the machete, Alden gripped it in his teeth to painstakingly hoist himself back aboard Burly.

On the trip back to the fire pit, Alden kept talking, and alternated holding the machete in his hand and his teeth to keep his mind thinking on the present moment and not his feverish distractions. Talking with the machete in his teeth gave him just that much more to concentrate on, and it all helped him maintain balance and pass the time. Every so often, he would look again at his right arm, and that would simultaneously shock him by its repulsive condition and remind him of the urgency of this task. The wound was a disgustingly inflamed ridge of seeping slime, and his arm and shoulder were so swollen that even as it hung in a resting state, his hand no longer touched his side. The pressure of resting the arm hurt him considerably, but so did trying to raise it away from the pressure. All he could do was switch from one epicenter of pain to the other, which he did, just for the variety.

They eventually arrived at the pit, and Alden slid off again, relieved in a small way that the task of staying aloft on Burly's back was over. Any relief for any reason was good. Short of breath, he rested, leaning on his left elbow. He knew better than to lie all the way down, as that could lead to losing consciousness, and he had a sense that any time that happened could be the last.

The pot of water he had carried there previously was still sitting next to one of the cinder block stacks, and the first thing to do was get it hoisted and ready over the fire area. Alden had not the slightest hope of accomplishing that himself, and the effort to prod his mind to formulate how to get Burly to help him was laborious. That, in turn, was discouraging, facing the circumstance that even thinking felt painful.

Alden crawled near the pot of water. Burly stayed close, moving with him. He reached up and pulled the end of the metal crossbar out of its hole in the block stack, and threaded it through the pot handle, so the far end was still up in its hole and the near end was angled down through the pot handle. Then, he sat on his haunches for a minute to rest and gather himself. Everything that took thought or action was exhausting.

"OK, Burly," Alden said weakly. He gestured in a short motion away from him, and Burly stepped to the opposite side of the cinder block stack.

"That's good, boy."

It would be easier if Burly could just pick up the bar in his teeth and lift it in place, but that was awkward. There was no room inside the pit for Burly's leg and head to fit and maneuver the bar without knocking the stack over. The melted halves of the original plastic tubes were still within reach, and Alden took one and mimed for Burly, placing one end under the metal bar and the other in his teeth.

Alden held the plastic tube out to his friend and the perceptive burlon responded immediately, grasping the end and placing the other under the bar, outside the pot handle. Alden wondered if Burly hadn't figured this one out by himself without the instructions. Burly lifted, but went a little too far.

"Whoa, boy," said Alden. He motioned downward with a flat hand, and Burly slowly lowered the bar until it was level and lined up with the proper hole. Alden raised his hand in a stopping gesture, then mustered a shove and poked the bar into the block. "That's it," he said, and Burly let the bar down and dropped the plastic tube.

The pot was still well off-center, and Alden thought a few moments about how to pantomime something that would get Burly to fix that, but he couldn't come up with anything. He let out a sigh and crawled slowly around the pit to the other side. Burly stayed there, and when Alden arrived he rose to his knees and reached up and silently patted the side of Burly's face. Then, he took the plastic tube and reached out with it to press the tip against the pot handle. That took several tries, but eventually he got it in place and started pushing on the plastic tube.

Burly now apparently understood what was up, because he snatched the plastic tube away from Alden and quickly used it to slide the pot out over the center of the fire pit.

"Wow, that's the way, boy," said Alden. Even in his stupor, he could still be impressed by the wherewithal of his companion, and it gave him a reassurance that he was not in this alone, and an odd sense that somewhere in that massive beast was the ability to miraculously take care of him.

Alden placed his shirt bandage and the machete in the pot, leaning the handle on the metal bar to keep it as far from heat as possible, and went to work building the twig teepee over dry leaves the way he'd done before. It was more of a challenge with one hand, but eventually it was ready. The sun was still high, and the lens made short work of the leaves. Within a few minutes, Alden had his precious fire blazing, quickly arranging the larger logs to make the largest inferno he could.

Next was waiting. Waiting was not just inconvenient; it was dangerous. Alden took a similar strategy as riding on Burly—talking. He also made himself crawl around the perimeter of the fire pit, resting when he must but only until he could crawl again. Burly was next to him the whole time, making a larger circle outside Alden's.

It was difficult to see into the pot from his knees, but after a while Alden could hear the bubbling. It worked. He was boiling water. He wasn't sure how long the machete would need to be in the water to be sterilized, but if the temperature of boiling water killed germs, it shouldn't need to be long. Also, the longer the boiling, the hotter the handle would be. He decided to leave the shirt bandage in the water to keep cleaning, but fetch the machete out and get the surgery over with.

He knelt high and reached quickly out over the fire to grab the machete. The handle was a little uncomfortable, but not burning him, and he snatched it out. He rolled back off his knees so he was sitting with his legs out in front of him. He was intensely scared about this, and breathing very quickly.

Alden was tearing up in anticipation of what this might feel like, and he placed the blade of the machete lightly on the surface of the wound, at the bottom. Then he scraped it upward along the ridge of the gash. The pain was excruciating. He nearly fell over. But he had not broken the surface of the wound.

He began crying softly as he quickly placed the machete blade at the bottom again, intentionally not giving himself time to think about what this was going to feel like. His left hand was shaking, but with a determined motion, he dug the blade in firmly and made a rapid swipe up his arm, then dropped the machete.

Alden had not actually called out verbally from his pain very much so far. He'd never felt anything like what this injury had done to him, but for whatever reason—his own resolve, or trying not to worry Burly, or whatever else he was discovering about his natural countenance—he had not yelled from the pain. Not until that moment.

Alden screamed in torment. Burly lifted his head and bellowed a sympathetic wail in concert.

Tears streaming, Alden looked down at his arm and all the repulsive white goo oozing from it. It filled his snotting nostrils with the foul stench of decay. As if from reflex to flush the poison from inside, he reached to it and squeezed. He screamed again, stabbed with unspeakable agony, as he watched mounds of horrid-smelling infection gush from the wound. Battling the torture with determination, he moved his left hand up and down his arm, pushing and clutching until all the fluids he saw through weeping eyes were either red or clear.

Then, he flopped backward on the ground and passed out.

❖

Alden's eyes opened wearily. Staying on his back, he lifted his left hand to his face and wiped it. He heard Burly groan softly.

"Hi, boy," Alden said with a crackling, dry voice.

He rolled to his left to push up to a sitting position. His right arm hurt, and was covered in dried blood, but his chest was normal size again. The surgery was a success.

The sun was a little farther in the sky, but Alden was in shade, thanks to Burly standing to cast his shadow. Alden glanced in the fire pit and noticed the logs were ash and the pile was cold. That couldn't have happened in just the hour or two indicated by the sun's movement. He'd been out for at least one whole day. Maybe more. No way to know.

What he did know was he had no sunburn, meaning Burly had stood by him the entire time, blocking the sun all day long.

"Burly, my friend," said Alden, "you took real good care of me. Thanks, buddy."

With stiff, creaking joints, Alden moved to get himself up on his knees. His right arm still wasn't worth much to push or hold things, but it was far from the source of constant torture it had been. He slowly bent the elbow to test it. It felt a bit squishy, and his lower arm had some swelling. The wound itself was a mess, with dried blood and ragged edges. All in all, though, the pain didn't change much with the movement. This was a huge improvement.

Alden's thoughts were clear, and his balance seemed stable, so he decided to try to stand. With deliberation, he placed his left foot out in front of him, rested his left hand on his knee, leaned his weight forward, and gave a shove. He was weak. He took several wobbly steps to stay right, but found himself and stood erect for the first time in days. How many, he would never be sure exactly.

Burly moved from his shading position and turned his head to Alden, who laid his left hand on Burly's snout and rubbed lightly.

"We're gonna be OK, boy," Alden said. "I think we're gonna be OK."

Alden reached out with his right hand and laid it on the outside of the water pot.

"Cold. Not much in there anymore, either." He took his left hand and reached in. "It must still be clean, though, eh, boy? You didn't spit in here or anything, did you?"

He took out the wet shirt bandage and squished some water out of it, as best he could with mostly one hand. He did some wiping on his arm, clearing away the bulk of the dried seepings. It hurt, and he might have thought a lot but for comparison to the condition it was in before. Then, he rolled the shirt as a bandage the way he did before, and got it tied around the arm. Even with the pain, the cool pressure of the wet shirt felt good. A helpful, healing pain.

"Burly, pal," said Alden as he finished the knot, "I need to get clean bad and all that, but first I need more rest, and some water down below. I'm gonna lie down and sleep some more. You've been here so good and so long, watchin' over me. Go get yourself a bunch of nice, refreshing water and some fruitleaf bushes. I'll be ready in the morning."

Burly groaned a little. Burly's noises never really

sounded like agreement or understanding, but by now Alden knew that's what they meant. He kind of took it as learning Burly's language in a way, the way he knew Burly probably understood more of what Alden said than he could realize.

Alden went to the cave opening and lowered himself down, encouraged that it was all thankfully easier than the last time climbing up. He paused when only his head was above the rim, and looked at Burly, who hadn't moved.

"It's all right, boy," he said. "You go on, now. I'm fine."

Alden disappeared to get a much-needed drink and healing sleep.

In the morning, Alden was awake at a much more normal time. He was also feeling more normal, and hungrily enjoyed two cans of food, corn and tuna. He could flex his right elbow without problems, and he figured he could use the hand for something like braiding vine rope, but climbing with it or swinging the hatchet was still too much.

Energy was an issue, too. Being on the mend and feeling more like himself was fabulous, but he was going to need some time to get his strength and stamina back. All of that was a welcome and happy circumstance, though, and Alden was thrilled just to be able to stand, climb out of the cave, and greet Burly coming from the forest.

"Hey there, buddy," said Alden as Burly strode up. Burly grunted and waved his snout at Alden's arm.

"Yeah, way better today. I'm gonna be tired today, but I'm gonna be alive, and that's the main thing. Ready to get started?"

Burly grunted again and waved his head, a little more animated than his usual responses. Alden patted his snout.

"Yeah, I'm happy, too, boy. Thanks for watching over me."

Alden climbed aboard and started the day with some much-needed chores. He was in his olive cargo shorts, blue T-shirt, and safari hat, and had his pouch packed with his standard equipment—hatchet, water bottle, and some clothes for washing. He was trusting that the machete belonged in the forest again, so he was carrying that until they got to the woods.

His time in the ravine stream was especially refreshing that morning, and he took extra to get everything rinsed over and over, including himself. He renewed his bandage and examined the cut. It was ragged, but improving. The redness and swelling were both way down.

Next was the garden, with some more carrots—some for Burly, some for the pouch—and some weeding. Alden needed to pace himself, so he didn't overdo things, but with his left hand he ran the hoe through some of the more overgrown areas.

Then it was off into the forest. Alden did get a lot of rope braided, and they took a trip in to the fruitleaf bushes, with a stop at the plateau stream to wash carrots. It occurred to Alden how strange it was that they were having a blessedly normal day, but one vastly different from a normal day just a few short weeks before. As much as he missed his parents, life on his own was taking on its unique signature. And in critical ways, it wasn't life on his own now; it was life with Burly. As sure as the daily blazing sun, they had attached themselves to one another, and in ways both obvious and hidden, that was keeping Alden alive.

With everything they'd been through already, though, the greatest challenge remained ahead.

Building a bridge.

Chapter 18

Over the next few days, Alden continued to mend, and soon found himself healthy enough to be fully active. The ankle was behaving normally and the arm was much closer, though there was considerable scabbing on the gash. It was feeling like a regular cut, though, with surface tightness and some occasional light seeping through cracks instead of the deep soreness and effects on his muscles. He kept his bandage on it, boiling the shirt every other day and stream washing it in between. Sometimes, when it pulled or stung a little, it prompted Alden as a reminder to scan the skies and make sure there were no predators circling, but he never saw one.

These things took time, and Alden had to make an effort to maintain the patience for it. He felt like he had some catching up to do, although they were on no schedule other than the ongoing urgency to make progress and get home. Alden remained driven. Much of what lay before him was a process of discovery, and Alden's curiosity for problem solving kept feeding that aspect of his personality.

Once he could climb with relative ease again, and had the first tree's vines all braided to rope, it was time to see about getting the fallen tree in the ravine put to good use. Chopping was expensive work, costing time and tiring effort, and if he could stand that tree up again it was far better than just replacing it with a new one.

Alden got down into the ravine and arranged some rope around the top of the tree. It had toppled into the thick ravine brush, but by crawling on top of it, he didn't have to fight his way through the dense foliage. When he had it secured, he took the other end of the lengthy cord and ascended the ladder to where Burly was waiting. With the rope fastened across Burly's neck plate the way it had been before for dragging, Alden began guiding Burly slowly in the right direction to hoist the tree where he wanted it.

The cable pulled tight, then groaned a little as Alden's braids settled under the tension, but it held, and then began moving.

"You OK, boy?" Alden said with his hand on Burly's side. Burly ignored the question and stepped slowly and smoothly forward.

For the first few feet, the tree just scooted along the floor of the ravine, so Alden stopped Burly until he could climb back down. He called to his friend to start again, and in another few feet he timed a great shove to get the bottom of the tree trunk to catch on one of the only two remaining pillars of the short portion of the bridge. Then, as Burly continued to pull, the top of the tree rose.

Alden scurried up the ladder, but only to where he

could reach over the top edge and grab another substantial length of vine rope. Burly pulled until the tree was vertical and right next to the bridge pillar, when Alden called to him again to stop. The pillar was very close to the ladder. With his legs wrapped securely within the frame of the ladder and the top of one foot hooked on a rung to steady himself, he reached out around the tree and made a pass around the tree and pillar, knotting it. The rope was a bit stiffer than when it was fresh, and working quickly was abrasive on Alden's hands, but he was too excited and too anxious to keep the tree where it stood to slow down.

He made two more passes, knotting each one. After the third pass and a sturdy knot, he had rope left over, but he let it dangle to be available for tying the next tree.

Alden let out a whoop, sprang up the top rungs of the ladder, and ran to Burly. Removing the rope harness, he hugged his companion around the back of his head.

"Come on, boy!" he said. "We did it—come look at this!"

He ran back to the bridge and Burly followed at a brisk walking pace. Alden gestured at the tree protruding four feet up from the bridge surface.

"We did it, boy!" Alden put his hands on the tree and tried to wiggle it. It stayed firm. "Our first one, Burly. Our first step to actually building our bridge. Isn't it great?"

Burly raised his head slightly and grunted.

"I know, I know, it took us long enough to get here, huh, boy," said Alden. "Let's go chop down another tree."

<❖>

Between building up strength and stamina and chores like tending to the garden, it was three more days, but Alden felled another tree and took to braiding the fresh vines. He was in a good, satisfied place, balancing the anxious energy of wanting to make progress with the comfort of simply being able to work each day. When it was time to drag the second tree to the bridge and tip it into the ravine, Alden was trying a new strategy of having a loose length of rope in place already between the top of the tree and Burly. After pushing the tree over the edge, Burly could back up and put tension on that rope, preventing the tree from toppling over as it had in their first attempt.

That worked well, and soon there was a second post tied in place, beginning the structure of their lifeline to the grassland.

The next morning, Alden put the bird talon in his pouch as he was preparing for the day. When he and Burly got to the bridge, he took it out and walked over to the wooden sign that still stood to the right of the bridge entrance. The sign had been placed there by the Sec Crew when the bridge was being built, as an amusement reflecting one of the crew's status as a short-timer, about to retire from Sec Crew work. His name was Basil, and the crew painted "Basil Bridge" in haphazard lettering. There was one on the far side of the ravine as well.

Alden held the talon in both hands and began scraping at the sign. The talon was plenty sharp enough to engrave deeply in the wood, and in a few minutes he was finished. He stepped back and gestured at it, addressing Burly.

"There we go, boy," he said. "Nobody'll ever see that, but we'll know what we put here. I like it."

He let out a satisfied sigh and looked at it once more. In prominent grooves across the face of the sign, "Basil" was scratched out, and above it was carved "Alden," so the sign read "Alden Bridge."

With the first two trees in place in the ravine, Alden

was content that his basic concept of getting trees into the pit and tying them in place would work, so he turned his strategy to considering the best approach for long-term construction. That meant letting some trees dry out before hauling them to the ravine. In particular, it meant figuring out how to get some of them squashed more flat while they dried.

Trees in the supporting structure would serve best in their naturally round shape, but when it came time to lay a surface to walk on, round trees would be problematic. If he could get them flattened out like the logs in his cave, it would be much easier to walk on them, and cover more territory with each tree trunk at the same time.

To flatten trees, he needed weight. His cave logs got flattened by being beneath another tree that fell on top, but trying to make that arrangement seemed difficult. There were plenty of loose, flat rocks in the open terrain, up to sizes Alden couldn't hope to budge, probably even with Burly helping. If he could find enough of them the right size to move and get propped up for leaning on tree trunks, he could start producing flatter walking boards.

Alden dove into that project, resolving to find just the right way to do it. He was going to need lots of flat trees, and his squashing method had to be the best he could arrange. He figured he could chop whole trees into three lengths each, each piece a bit over ten feet long. That would be the width of Alden Bridge—a couple feet narrower than what the Sec Crew built, but it only had to be wide enough for Burly, who was maybe seven feet across at the belly. Having paced the width of the ravine, Alden estimated it at two hundred feet. Trees were two feet wide at the base, but chopping them into three sections meant not all sections were as wide as that. He could average maybe thirty inches per squished plank.

That was eighty planks to cross the ravine, or twenty-seven trees to flatten. The tree his dad cut down took a month to dry out, so assuming he could only squish one tree at a time, that operation alone would be more than two years. He needed to get it right.

The rock terrain was flat, but not without ridges and levels that varied by a few inches in places. Alden needed to use those ridges for steadying trees while they were flattened. If he tipped a rock against a round tree on a flat surface, it would just roll out from under, so he needed a good location to place a tree where it would rest against one of the short ridges and stay put.

Alden and Burly wandered the rocky parts of the plateau, including the large area south of the house, where Alden had chased down clothing and cans of food. They scouted both for a good place to lay the trees and for the proper rocks to use for flattening. Rocks were easier to find. In the end, Alden decided to make his own ridge by lining up some of the rocks in a row, something he realized might have been an easier approach to begin with, but that was just part of his education in problem solving.

Dragging rocks was harder than trees, and Burly strained himself against their weight, but he was up to the task. At first, Burly seemed reluctant and unsure of what this was about, but Alden took a stick and tiny rock and showed him an example of what he had in mind. Alden couldn't tell if Burly really understood the plan or simply understood that Alden had one, but either way, Burly was more determined and energetic after that.

Since Alden could choose the location of the tree-squishing operation, it made sense to set it up close to the forest. Dragging the rocks was a one-time thing; dragging the trees would happen twenty-seven times. It took a week, with plenty of resting and carrot snacks for Burly, but eventually all the rocks were lined up and ready. There were no natural ridges in the rock surface close enough to the forest, and it was more important to have the right location than to use the natural rock formations, so Alden set up one row of small rocks to serve as treestops and a row of large ones to tip onto the trees.

Two days of chopping later, they had a brushtop to flatten. Alden quickly discovered that dragging rocks was simpler than getting them on top of a tree. He pondered and built little models and pondered some more, finally deciding to spend some time in the ravine to see what resources he had from the original bridge frame. That took days longer, as he needed to clear out a lot of the thick brush with his machete to see what had landed within. That was something Burly couldn't help with, and Alden sometimes found himself hacking so long his arms were too overexerted to climb back up the ladder. When that happened, he took a washing break to refresh himself in the stream, and before long his muscles were behaving themselves again.

In the end, he was rewarded for his efforts. Alden uncovered a lot more of the angle bracing like the bar over the fire pit, and he had ideas for how to put that to good use. For starters, he set two pieces of it to make rails leaning on the tree. Burly could drag the rocks up the rails and onto the tree trunk. By that time, the tree they'd started with was beginning to dry out some, and Alden was concerned that it wouldn't flatten enough, so it was back to the forest with his hatchet. Within another three days, they were working with a fresh brushtop, and finally had a tree flattening.

Alden was sleeping well. This was grueling work. Between all the business with the trees and rocks and ravine bushes, there was washing and tending to the garden, to say nothing of all the vines that came off the felled trees and needed to be braided before they lost their pliability. These were long days, and Alden became more and more grateful that Burly never seemed to miss a beat. He was there for anything and everything Alden could ask. Alden wasn't discouraged—not yet—but when every task seemed to take days to resolve, it was sinking in that twenty-seven months of flattening trees, all while cutting more and tying them into a frame in the ravine, wasn't just a number. It was a very long time.

Chapter 19

As the work days wore on, Alden was becoming more acclimated to the idea of what daily life was really going to be. It was one thing to fight through the early adversity and promise Burly they were going to get home—all with the very best intentions—and another to wake up every day knowing that every muscle in his body was going to be spent by bedtime, and along the way would be hours spent on the simple maintenance of life. Resources and activities were sprawled out all over, and it was tough to fight the feeling that all the traveling required was a waste of time.

There was a relentless reality that every time he was finished with one thing and ready to tackle the next, he faced a quarter-mile hike to go do it. That was one of the things he was most grateful for with Burly. That blessed animal never batted an eye about trudging between the forest and the ravine, the ravine and cave, to the garden, to the fruitleaf bushes, anywhere. Burly was so big it seemed the walking had to somehow be difficult, but he had such grace about him that he made it seem effortless. He even sometimes galloped on their trips across the open rock, which never failed to invigorate them both. Strangely, Alden had to remind himself from time to time that Burly's whole existence was survival in the open, that he never had a life where transitioning from sleep to a meal was stepping out of the bedroom into the kitchen. For that matter, such a life was already like remembering a dream, even to Alden.

It all made for unusual juxtapositions of emotions for Alden in that every trip down into the ravine included the inescapable reminder of his father's crashed buggy laying in the brush, yet Alden routinely dismissed it in his mind as just another feature of the landscape. The same was true of the house foundation. He hadn't made a conscious decision that dwelling on the past would eat away at his resolve to survive, but that was his frame of mind nevertheless. Alden didn't cry very much about his parents anymore. The sting of missing them was acute, and in some ways every moment of his life was now a reminder that they were gone. At the same time, his circumstances were so incredibly different that he was disassociating with his previous life more and more completely. Emotionally, he had substituted Burly for his parents, and that allowed him to concentrate on looking ahead instead of wallowing in despair about his loss.

These things came a little closer to the surface when Alden was performing tasks such as hacking through the thick bushes of the ravine to uncover metal fragments from the old bridge frame. He maintained a healthy distance from the crashed buggy—maybe twenty feet—

but not because emotions were welling and he thought about how close he could get without bringing back startling memories of the day of the murders. It was more of an instinctual thing. Without even considering it, he knew exactly when he was as close as he was going to go. No need to think about going closer or why. Just don't do it.

The metal bars Alden found in the ravine were having a positive impact on his design of the bridge. He was realizing that sometimes working through difficult situations meant considerable extra work, but it was nice to make beneficial discoveries through that work. The pieces of metal meant his frame didn't need to be all tree trunks. Burly was available to help bend them straighter, and they made excellent rails not just for the rocks to flatten trees into planks, but to hold those planks on the bridge. Alden would be able to anchor metal rails extending from the existing support structure, then place planks on them. It meant that instead of having to get the vertical tree posts in place first for each small section of the bridge, he could extend the planks first, and work on a plank platform to tie the posts and braces in place. This was quite a boon to the operation, and it gave him more confidence that there were would be fewer risks and problems once he had made a couple of sections and had the process down.

In order to start that process, though, he needed planks, and that meant several weeks of letting his squishing tree squish under the rocks. In those weeks, Alden chopped more trees for posts and braces, braided lots and lots of vines, and tended the garden, including firing up the irrigation pump to get everything soaked again. The green button on the pump did exactly what he thought and hoped. Ever since he'd shut the pump down, there was the hanging question of getting it started again, so it was reassuring to have that answered.

Alden even played in the forceful blast from the irrigation tube, and got Burly to walk in front of it just to see what his enormous friend would do. Once again exceeding Alden's expectations, Burly actually seemed intrigued by water forcibly flowing the way it did from the pipe. He was drinking from the tube and entertaining Alden by letting the surge of water hit his bony neck collar and spray in all directions. Alden knew Burly had the capacity to think and care, and suspected he had fun when they ran together, but now he knew there was the ability to just plain play. There had been moments of victory and excitement in their endeavors, but simple laughter had been conspicuously rare. Playing with Burly in the water was a revelation that cemented a new layer of strength in their bond.

There was no perfect way for Alden to know how soon he could take the rocks off the flattening tree without risking some rebound to a rounder shape. He surmised that taking a few off the wider end would be the worst case and would only risk part of the tree if that portion rose up a little and then hardened, so at the three-week mark he had Burly help him shove some of the rocks away. The next day, it was already noticeably puffier there, so the rocks went right back on and Alden noted that it was likely to be a full month before he could use planks.

With that, it became obvious to Alden that other parts of the operation were going to get ahead of flattening planks. Early on, it wouldn't matter a lot; they could easily use as many trees as Alden could chop down while the first few trunks were compressing. But six or eight or eleven flat trees down the road, Alden could be faced with days with nothing constructive to do, bizarre as that notion seemed at the moment. That was a problem.

Setting up a second station for flattening trees was a

problem, too. Rocks the right size were easy enough to find the first time around, but it did take some searching, and Alden was concerned that there weren't enough good rocks available for a second flattening operation. Also, any and all acceptable rocks were farther away than the farthest one Burly dragged already, and that was taxing.

In the end, Alden decided to postpone a decision about it and see how things went, but he knew he might have to ask Burly to do some seriously strenuous hauling. Time was their worst enemy, and avoiding that difficult work at the expense of possibly weeks in the construction schedule was an inadvisable trade. Alden was willing to wait until after the first few rounds of planks were in place, to make sure that was going to go the way it should. No sense putting in all that exhausting work if they were to discover something drastically wrong with the plan. But they—meaning mostly Burly—could have a huge job ahead of them in a while, one more strenuous than anything they needed to do with trees.

In another week, Alden and Burly yanked the rocks off the thick end of the tree trunk, and the next day there was no change. It stayed put. Alden could move ahead with setting planks on the bridge.

As soon as they could slide the rocks away and move the flat tree, they dragged another in its place and hoisted the rocks onto it. There was no time to lose between flattening sessions. Once that was accomplished, Alden could turn to processing their new, flat tree trunk.

First was chopping it into three pieces. Alden had waited to do that so he could compare whether or not it was more difficult to chop a dried tree than a fresh one. It was harder to chop dry, but in the end it was faster. While the cured wood had more strength, it was also less flexible, and with it flat, all he had to do was score the tree and have Burly stomp to break it where Alden created a groove.

Within this project—and mode of living, for that matter—where everything was done with crude and makeshift methods and materials, making the bridge planks that way allowed for a refreshing bit of precision. Setting the lengths of the planks let Alden make them all the same, which meant more predictability in where and how the vertical support posts could go in place. The purpose of the bridge was clearly functional, but as long as it was better for functionality to have some consistency in the planks, it also didn't hurt that the whole thing would seem just that much less haphazard. A touch of neatness helped Alden feel like he was somehow doing it right. A small thing, but any contribution to a motivating, optimistic attitude could not be discounted.

Having a set length for planks also meant there would be some left over at the top of each tree, and smaller pieces would come in handy. They'd burned a lot of the available house shards in the fire pit, and there was plenty of very old, dry wood lying on the forest floor, but those were round and difficult to chop through. Flattened pieces Burly could break up by stomping made for much quicker processing into firewood.

With the one last week the first flat tree required to fully dry, something else was affecting their schedule: the annual blooming of the ravine bushes. It was late June, and that was the time of year the ravine became a teeming wave of light blue flowers. Hordes of insects and huge flocks of feeding birds came through the ravine during the bloom. Not the enormous, black, predatory birds; these were bug-eaters. They included the blue birds and the brown redheads Alden was used to seeing in the plateau forest, but also several other types. Small, black, stout birds with orange tips on their wings; sleek, purple birds with red crowns sticking up from their heads; and larger, multicolored birds in green and yellow, with some dashes of red and blue, seemingly for accent. Under different circumstances, Alden would have spent hours watching and listening to the vibrant display of nature. As it was, he took breaks to admire the annual scene, but for the most part he was simply annoyed that he was displaced from the ravine stream during the two weeks of blooming. He had to go all the way into the woods to the spring pond and forest stream for his daily chores.

Alden probably could have worked at the bridge height during that time, but it seemed unnecessarily risky. If he dropped anything, he couldn't retrieve it, and—worse—if he fell in, it could be disastrous, even if he managed to land in the bushes like last time. Also, while the insects stayed low to the plants, the birds swooped all over the place. Alden didn't want to spend time over the ravine trying to work and stay out of the way of the dive-bombing wildlife at the same time, possibly making errors with both. It just didn't seem like a good idea.

As the blooming activity was tapering off, Alden eagerly turned his attention to the bridge frame, and laid the first three cut planks on the metal rails. He tied a weave of rope around the ends and the rails, to hold the planks in place. Because of the tapering from the base of the tree trunk to the top, the planks did not have parallel sides, but it was a simple matter to alternate the wider ends. Also, the planks were slightly thicker down one edge than the other due to the angle of the leaning rocks. Balancing rocks directly on top of the trees was far too difficult, and leaning the rocks on the trees made them into somewhat of a wedge, but the variation was small. Alden nevertheless pieced the thicker and thinner portions together between each plank, creating a smooth transition between. The surface of the bridge would therefore fluctuate up and down slightly over its length, but without any hard edges. Besides the satisfaction in Alden's mind of optimizing the design with the available materials, it would be important for trees and feet not to catch on edges as they dragged or pushed things repeatedly down the bridge.

With planks in place on the metal rails, it was time to tip two more vertical tree posts over the edge and secure those to the rails as well. Positioning was not precise, but there was little Alden could do about that. Once a tree was standing up in the ravine, he could lean it one way or another, but moving the location of the base on the ravine floor was too difficult. He tried a few times to rotate a tree and get the base to swivel to a better position, but it was awkward. To do that, he had to stand on the bridge and reach out around the tree trunk to hug it, then rotate it. The trees were much too heavy for that, and it was going to be too easy for Alden to lose his own balance and fall into the ravine. He would have to rely on improving the technique for tipping trees over the edge, because once they landed, there they were.

Setting the planks and posts took a week, and over the next three, while the second tree was flattening, Alden did a lot of chopping, braiding, and gardening. He mixed up his schedule better, so the chopping wouldn't wear him out so much. His young muscles didn't develop and tone the way older men's did, and although soreness became less of an issue through the constant use, fatigue was something he had to learn to manage.

As for the gardening, Alden was harvesting and cooking green beans a lot. He knew the beans couldn't stay on the plants too long, and he picked them all for storage in the cave. He had a couple muskmelon vines, and those came in as well. Alden loved fruit, and melons were a particular treat. Burly thought so, too, and between them, the crop only lasted a few days, but that was better than having anything spoil.

The corn was close but not quite ready. The carrots were long gone, but the seed plants were doing well and he'd be able to plant more soon. It was a week since Alden polished off the last of his canned food, so the garden was an important activity. It always had been, and he knew that, but now he was actually feeling it. The fruitleaf bushes were an acceptable food source, but Alden was not relishing the idea that it could ever be his only food source. As evidenced by the discovery of the fruitleaf plants in an area of the plateau his family had never seen, there was still plenty of acreage to explore, and it was possible some other food source might be out there. That would be a major project of its own, though. For the time being, he was content to eat fruitleaves supplemented with garden fare, concentrating on getting the bridge built. That was the top priority.

Chapter 20

Alden awoke and prepared himself for the day the way he had almost every day for the past five months. Dressing himself wasn't a lot different, but Alden could tell he'd better be ready to make some adjustments before too long. He'd grown some. His T-shirts had always been pretty large and they were still OK, but he was going to need a pair of his father's shorts soon. Tan cargo shorts the same style as his olive pair. Dad's pants were way too big, but too big was better than too small, and he was already thinking about fixing up a pair of suspenders from brushtop vines. Shoes were going to be an issue, also. He could still wear his, but they were getting tight. He had three pairs of socks, though one didn't match, and a couple of single shoes from his folks—Dad's right shoe and Mom's left. He tested the fit and discovered if he wore four socks to fit into his dad's shoe and two to fit the other, he could make that work when he needed to.

With a fruitleaf breakfast, and tools and water packed in his pouch, he climbed up to meet Burly, and it was off to the ravine for washing. It was another clear, sunny day, but unusually windy, so much so that Alden thought he might blow off of Burly once or twice. It was also strange that the wind was coming from the south, blowing from the house foundation straight into the edge of the forest. On windy days, it was normally the opposite direction, or some angle across the ravine and the open rock terrain.

Alden was very happy with how things were working out in the ravine. He had six trees' worth of planks installed, making over forty feet of bridge. It was sturdy, and Alden had to admit he was impressed with himself. He was actually building a real, working bridge across this ravine. Imagining it and planning it and promising it were all one thing; seeing it stand in front of him was entirely different.

The most difficult part was the bracing. For strength and stability, vertical posts alone weren't enough. He proved that to himself with his twig models when he first set out to design the framework. There must be braces at angles along the sides and between posts beneath the planks. Those braces intersected with the vertical posts at various locations in their height, which meant both Alden and the bracing tree had to be somehow suspended in place for him to tie it properly.

Holding the tree in place was Burly's job. Burly could stand with a vine rope attached to him and the tree, and slowly lower it down until it was where Alden wanted. After that, Alden had to get down to tie the joint. He fixed that by creating his own hanging ladder from shards of dried brushtop wood and vine rope. With a safety rope around his waist and connected to Burly, he climbed down the ladder to the joint. The safety rope came into the picture after a close call; Alden lost his balance and nearly plunged off the ladder and into the ravine. After that, he started using the safety rope, and smartly so. Not a week later, he slipped all the way off the ladder. Only once, and it was no fun hanging by his waist while Burly hauled him up, but it was better than the alternative.

The result of all the climbing and tying, chopping and squishing and dragging, was a structure that was immensely satisfying. Watching it take shape was in many ways equivalent to success itself, and that kept his morale high and motivation fueled. He could even sense the anticipation in Burly each time they walked out to the end of the bridge, forty feet into the ravine, where they could see and feel the other side just that little bit closer.

Alden got himself and his clothing washed up. The atmosphere in the ravine felt restless, as the angle of the winds whipped straight up the ravine corridor, constantly rustling the bushes. It was generally quiet in the ravine, even when there were breezes up top, and the gale gusts made things colder and more difficult than usual.

Dressed and ready for work, Alden climbed up to the bridge surface. Burly was there, and the two set off for a day of regular chores. Alden spent the trip with one arm flopped over his safari hat, to keep it on his head in the stiff winds.

Just before they reached the outer edge of the garden, Burly abruptly lurched up and Alden was thrown off to his right. He landed without injury, feeling immediately that it wasn't Burly who did the lurching. The ground was heaving and vibrating. It was another earthquake.

Burly went down on his left side, and Alden couldn't tell if it was on purpose or not. He tried momentarily to get up and go to him, but quickly fell again. The shaking was violent, and got more so.

Alden lay on his back, hoping that was his safest position, but he was being tossed all the way in the air a few inches by the convulsions beneath him, and landing on the rock was jarring. He held his hat on, both because of the wind and to try to protect his head from impact.

The jolts continued for what seemed like minutes, first up and down then side to side then throwing Alden in the air again. He turned his head enough to look at Burly, but all he could see was bouncing. No movement; Burly was limp. Alden could only hope that was Burly's tactic to wait out the quake, just as it was his, since neither of them had much choice yet. Alden was thinking it would have been nice to at least get to the forest first, where there was a layer of dead foliage and some dirt to cushion the blows of being pounded onto the rock.

Eventually, the heaving subsided to tremors, and Alden was maintaining contact with the ground. He immediately tried to get up again and get to Burly, and fell down twice in the attempt, but when he was able to keep his footing and stand, something else froze him in place.

The near edge of the forest was gone.

Every single brushtop in the first five hundred feet of the forest, where they were less dense against the wind, had blown over. They looked like dominoes someone had toppled, or enormous hair that had been combed to the ground.

Alden was dumbfounded. He stood and gaped at the devastation.

In another moment, he snapped out and turned to Burly, who was moving to get his feet back under him.

"Burly!" said Alden. "Burly! Are you OK?"

Burly was managing all right under the circumstances and didn't seem to be hobbling as he stood. He let out a mournful groan.

"Are you hurt, boy?" Alden said, placing a hand on his snout.

Burly grunted, and Alden knew that time he was fine, and the earlier noise was just a general complaint about the event. The ground was still rumbling off and on, but had quieted down.

"Burly, look at this," Alden said as he gestured out to all the fallen trees. There were hundreds.

"Holy cannoli. This is ... this is amazing."

Alden's head was racing with what this meant for their lives, both good and bad.

The good: no more chopping, except to get fresh trees to flatten.

The bad: everything else. The trees would no doubt have destroyed the water pipeline completely. Irrigating the garden was a thing of the past. All access to the forest was blocked by this blanket of brushtops, so there was no fruitleaf food or water at all for Burly until they could clear at least a narrow path between the trees. That could mean dragging a dozen of them out into the open rock. Alden could still easily see trees that were standing, and that told him they may not have fallen deep enough in the forest to cause a problem blocking the forest stream from the spring pond, but that might be wishful thinking. Pessimistic thinking would consider that the spring itself could have been closed or permanently changed by the earthquake, and that would be disastrous.

Thinking of disasters, Alden suddenly screamed.

"The bridge!"

He turned and sprinted, his hat falling away and blowing into the low foliage near the garden. Burly charged up behind and quickly overtook Alden, who paused just long enough to jump on board, knowing Burly was faster. Burly galloped the entire distance into the howling winds, huffing and panting as they approached a monumentally catastrophic scene.

Alden was stricken. Battered to the core by what he saw.

Every tree, every plank, every stitch of braided rope was in the bottom of the ravine. All of it.

Utterly defeated, Alden slid off of Burly and walked onto the short piece of the original bridge, now once again all that was left. He sank woefully to his knees, then leaned forward onto his hands.

Alden screamed a long, tormented wail.

In unison, Burly lifted his head and belted a mighty howl of lament.

Alden began crying, stabbed to the heart of his very identity by this horrific turn. There were no words for the desolation of his emotions. Everything he had done—all of the work he and Burly had slaved over for months, fighting through injury and illness and the oblivion of survival—wiped asunder in two minutes.

He suddenly rose and turned to face away from the ravine. He raised two clenched fists next to his head and screamed again, long and hard. With a quick thought, he strode with determination to the sign reading "Alden Bridge," which had ironically endured the shaking. He gave the post two forceful side kicks with his left leg, and it snapped off and toppled into the ravine.

Immediately, Alden walked away, toward the house wreckage. It was more instinctive than purposeful, born of terror that he might do something unforgiveable if he stayed near the ravine. When his parents were murdered, he stopped himself from jumping in. The urge to jump, to thrown himself down with the destruction, was strong again, but the urge to stop was nowhere to be found.

Alden still had the capability of realizing that Burly's days would be short if he ended his right then and there, but whether that was bad or good was murky. Maybe he should just put Burly out of his misery. Maybe this was a doomed effort from the start. Making promises to Burly proved to be supremely foolish, and anything from this point would just be leading Burly on.

What was he thinking, anyway, trying to build a bridge? He was eleven, traipsing around with a prehistoric beast he thought was his friend, but what if that's not even real? What if all of this was a dream? Could he even really do this? Could he chop down trees and build fires and grow a garden? Really?

The concept of starting over was just so devastating Alden couldn't grasp it. He blocked it out. His mind went back to the happy life. He thought of running around with Dad to take plant samples, and eating cherry pie with Mom, and playing Bagadon Warrior, the game with his favorite character Thalok in it. No thoughts of crops or flattened trees or braided rope. No terrifying black birds or delirium-inducing infections.

No murdered parents.

Just an adventure of pioneering discovery.

He continued wandering past the house in the direction of his cave, completely oblivious to virtually everything, including Burly just behind him to his left. Alden's pummeled mind was closed. In his stupor, his only thought was to climb into the cave and stay. As he approached, however, he was startled back toward reality in a most shocking way.

His cave was gone, too. The roof of the entire cavern had collapsed in the earthquake, crumbling in on top of all of Alden's belongings. There was no shelter. No escape.

Alden collapsed to the ground near the edge of what used to be the entrance hole to his cave, and sat. He was completely stunned. Beyond crying. Beyond caring.

Burly licked Alden's left arm. The sensation registered, but the meaning didn't.

"Go away," Alden said plainly.

Burly didn't leave, but he didn't lick again, either.

After a minute or two, Alden simply flopped over on his side and retreated completely into sleep.

The sun was higher when Alden opened his eyes, but not a lot. He wasn't positive exactly where it was in the sky, because Burly was making a shadow on him again. Alden immediately saw the collapsed cave, and it brought everything back from before his nap.

"Geez, Burly, don't you ever get sick of being with me?" Alden said. "Go on." Alden waved toward the forest. "Get outa here. Go get yourself—"

He paused with the realization that there was nowhere for Burly to go, no way for him to get into the forest. Alden burst into tears.

He was coming face to face again with his responsibility to Burly, and it weighed heavily. This was all too much for a boy. People were supposed to be taking care of him, not him taking care of himself and a wild animal who, powerful as he may be, depended on Alden now. Alden didn't feel dependable. He felt crushed, and alone, and deeply angry at the unfairness of his lot.

Alden stood, sniffled, and began walking toward the forest.

"Come on, ya dumb animal," he said. Burly grunted, and Alden stopped and turned to him.

"I'm sorry, Burly. You're the most amazing thing I've ever seen. I just wish I could get past feeling like if you weren't here, I'd be dead and happy of it. I know you don't deserve this. Any more than I do. It's just right now you're a big, fat pain. Let's go."

Alden walked off, and Burly followed, just behind him to his left. Alden grumbled under his breath, "Somebody's gonna pay for this."

They trudged away in the direction of the garden, Alden on his feet the whole time. He was too upset to ride, and the walking felt more like he was either working out frustration or building it up. He wasn't sure which.

Chapter 21

Their first stop was retrieving the safari hat so Alden could work in the sun. It had blown across the garden and up against a fallen brushtop. Alden hadn't noticed the first time, when he was distracted by the spectacle of the leveled forest, but all the corn was completely flat. He'd planted another round as soon as he could after the previous harvest; they both enjoyed the corn. The new crop wasn't fully matured, but close, and would work just fine. Guess it was time to harvest. When he got around to it.

The trees weren't as thick of a blanket as they looked from farther away, though the mass of fresh vines created somewhat of a thicket that took some navigation. Even so, Alden and Burly were making quick work of just rolling trees out of the way in a path toward the spring pond. After a half dozen of them, Alden stopped and put his hands on his hips.

"I'll bet you knew you could do this yourself, didn't you, boy. You just wanted to get me up and moving. It won't work, ya know." He walked away toward the next tree and muttered to himself, "Dumb animal, my eye."

Within ninety minutes, they'd worked their way to where the first few trees were still standing, and not long after that, they could walk between the downed trunks the rest of the way. By the time they reached the spring pond, they were well into undamaged forest again.

At the pond, Alden got the first bit of positive news from all this: the water seemed to be flowing from the pond out into the forest stream in a normal way, meaning the spring was not closed by the earthquake. That would have been unspeakably disastrous. Alden and Burly both drank their fill and continued out to the fruitleaf bushes for lunch.

Alden's emotions were conflicted and tumultuous. As he worked with Burly to clear their way through the devastation, he was following through on everything with commitment, but there was no enthusiasm or sense of purpose. He was simply resigned to proceeding with helping Burly stay alive, and that to no good end. It was just so he wouldn't feel completely disgusted with himself at abandoning his responsibility. Alden was sure that all he was doing was delaying their inevitable deaths on the plateau, creating a perception that he was trapped in a supremely meaningless existence.

When they were finished eating, Alden looked around without direction.

"Well, what now, Burly?" he said. "You should probably just stay here in the forest. You got food and water here. Heck, as far as that goes, so should I. There's nothing waiting for me out on the rock anymore."

It was very strange, but for the first time Alden felt like

he had nothing to do. He was not interested in starting back into any construction or salvage activity. That was just work for the sake of work, and they'd busted their butts enough already, with nothing to show for it. Less than nothing, with his cave gone. Working on the bridge would have simply driven home his sense of defeat.

"Tell you what," said Alden with an idea. "Let's explore. No time like the present. Let's see what else is on the plateau before we die. Whatcha think?"

Burly offered no response at all. Alden had never felt so disconnected from his friend. From everything. He was going through the motions, bitterness overwhelming his countenance.

Alden climbed onto Burly, and although Burly seemed less than enthusiastic, he went where Alden guided, back to the forest stream and across it, to the huge northeast areas of the plateau. Alden had never been to these parts of the forest. If Burly had, it was either before they met or at night, but since Burly was always back by morning, he couldn't have gotten terribly far.

Most of the foliage was made up of things they'd seen before. At first it was thick, but eventually it became more sparse. They went on at a slow, ambling pace for hours, until the sun was low. Alden didn't speak much, just watching the landscape go by and thinking about their situation. He could feel it was unfair to take any of this out on Burly, but it was such an incredibly raw deal he wasn't in a frame of mind for graciousness. Not yet.

They were much too far away from the southern rock terrain to go back before nightfall, and Alden was quite seriously in touch with his observation that there was nothing to go back for, anyway, so he slid down from Burly, picked a spot where he could sit back on an old, fallen brushtop, and nodded off for the night.

◄❖►

Morning was odd, not being in his cave, and miles from it to boot. Burly was nowhere to be seen. Alden thought that was fitting, especially with how cold Alden had been to him, and he wondered if Burly had simply wandered off to be on his own. Not like they wouldn't cross paths now and then—the plateau was big, but water was in only one place—but Alden was considering he might be left to live out his miserable days by himself. Maybe he'd reconsider throwing himself into the ravine, here in the north end of the plateau.

Alden took the last drink from his water bottle and started walking in the direction he and Burly were the evening before. He was shoving bushes out of his way from time to time, but it was pretty easy navigating. The wind was far less violent than the disaster the day before, and the sweet scent of the brushtops settled strongly on the forest floor.

After a short time, Alden heard, then felt, a familiar thumping on the ground. Looking ahead, he saw Burly trotting toward him. In that moment, things felt more like they used to, and that was a welcome flash of normalcy. It simultaneously struck Alden as happy and sad—happy to see Burly, sad that it immediately reminded him of how things would never be the old way again.

In another moment, Burly was in front of him.

"Hey, boy," Alden said. Like so often before, Alden would have put a hand on Burly's snout except for the mild huffing and twitching Burly always had when he'd been exerting himself. Alden was deeply pleased to hear Burly's brief snorts and have his companion with him again. He hadn't wanted to be on his own; he just needed to be prepared for it, and thought it would be an appropriate place for his life to go.

Burly tossed his head to one side.

"You find somethin', boy?" Alden happily climbed

aboard, and Burly turned and walked briskly back toward where he'd been.

Before long, Alden could see a brighter area ahead, somewhere the brushtops were thinner and more sunlight reached the ground. As they approached, he also noticed a new kind of vegetation dotting the forest. Trees about ten feet tall, with stout branches and broad, green leaves, sprinkled among the brushtops. He was also struck by the sounds he began to hear—birds chirping. Lots and lots of birds.

The sound became louder, then almost deafening as an awful smell took hold in the air. They came upon a vast area of the new trees. The brushtops didn't just get thinner. They stopped, in an abrupt line at the edge of this tumultuous territory. Brushtops were absent here, replaced by a new forest utterly alive with birds—thousands upon thousands of both the blues and the redheads. Thick with nests, these woods looked more like baskets with leaves. Birds were coming and going at a maniacal pace. It was bedlam.

"Holy cannoli," said Alden quietly.

Burly had stopped next to a brushtop, one very near the edge of the bird territory where there were only the nesting trees, and Alden was thankful for that as he looked around at the ground. The bird habitat was blanketed in a disgusting layer of poop that kept him from wanting to get any closer.

He watched as the symphony of nature raged before him, oblivious to the two outsiders, the burlon and human who didn't belong on the plateau. This was the domain of the flighted.

"So, this is where they all live. Wow."

After a few moments more, Alden wanted to move along and see what else there was in the unexplored regions of this unique habitat of Cappa Terse. He gave Burly a tap, and Burly began walking, remaining within the brushtops and skirting the edge of the bird woods. Soon, they were passing the far end of it, and the incredible din of the massive flocks began to fade away.

Alden was happy for the diversion, something to take his mind off their situation for a few minutes. It really was quite a phenomenon. He was also happy to be enjoying a more normal feeling of riding Burly through the woods. Upset though he was, he felt silly for having alienated his companion. That wasn't right. Friends are supposed to go through tough times together.

The brushtop forest remained much as it was on the more familiar side of the stream, and before long— sooner than Alden expected—they reached the eastern edge of the ravine. That, too, was largely the same as along the west edge.

"Well, I guess that's about that for our discoveries, eh, Burly?" Alden said. "Nothin' new to eat or drink out here, and you must be starved. Let's get back to the spring pond."

They circled around through the eastern forest to approach the pond from the opposite side to the normal path. Thankfully, they did come across a small patch of fruitleaf bushes, where they stopped for some needed lunch. The spring pond was a welcome sight when they finally arrived, and Burly and Alden both drank heartily.

Alden patted Burly's snout.

"Seems I keep havin' to say this, but I'm sorry, boy. Sorry I got mad at you. I know none of this is your fault. I just don't know what to do. It's a mess. I'm still really angry at losin' everything, but I'll do my best not to take it out on you."

He paused, and his eyes were watering. Alden really didn't know what to do. He felt deeply lost and ill-equipped to make any decisions in the face of the devastation of all they'd worked toward.

"So, are we OK? We still friends?"

Burly tossed his head a little and grunted. Alden smiled.

"I knew we would be. You're good that way."

Alden climbed aboard.

"I guess we oughta go take a look at the cave. More like the cave-in now. See if there's stuff we can save from there."

Burly headed south, and as if Alden needed a reminder, the scope of the damage struck him freshly again as they followed their makeshift path between all the fallen brushtops. Alden was silently stunned, not only by revisiting their misfortune, but by the power of nature required to topple all those trees.

The open rock terrain felt more familiar, and Alden helped himself to some water from his bottle and a few remarks to Burly about how they were both getting bounced around during the quake. Alden wasn't quite ready to joke about it, but just talking about it was a way to help deal with it.

Finally, they pulled up at the demolished cave. Alden noticed that the fire pit stacks of cinder blocks had toppled over, but that was the least of his worries. He slid down off Burly and stepped over to the ladder at the old cave entrance. It was actually still attached, giving Alden a way to let himself down into the mess of crumbled stone.

He didn't climb in immediately. He stood at the edge looking down, noticing a few items of clothing and such between the broken rocks.

"You know what, Burly?" he said thoughtfully. "I could've been in there. You know what else?" He paused, measuring his words carefully before he chose to say them out loud.

"If Mom and Dad were alive, and none of that happened, I would have been. If I didn't have a bridge to build or clothes to wash, I'd have been out here doin' stuff in my cave." He thought for another few moments. "And you know what? Mom and Dad would still be alive. They'd be alive, without me, Burly. They'd be sick. I know them."

Alden began crying softly, his voice wavering as he fought to finish his thoughts.

"They loved me, Burly. They always got so scared if they thought I was hurt, or lost. I could never leave them like that."

He thought for another moment, and sniffled.

"This is better."

Chapter 22

Knowing that the earthquake would have occurred regardless of his circumstances, the idea that Alden might actually prefer this situation over one where his parents had not been murdered was an astounding revelation. Thinking he would have been in his cave when it collapsed was an assumption, and perhaps a poor one, but even the possibility of it changed everything in Alden's mind. He not only accepted his lot, he welcomed it.

Alden didn't entirely rule out the notion that he might have ultimately preferred to be rescued by the supply ship, or even killed with his parents, but he remained aware that both of those scenarios left Burly alone on the plateau. He had a remarkable connection with Burly, and the purpose of that in his and in Burly's life could not be discounted.

With this, Alden's mind became unencumbered by the burden that this was a cruel and defeating twist of fate. Rather, it was the way things were supposed to be. Moreover, the way he wanted them. Instead of being a nail in the coffin—or perhaps more like a railroad spike—the earthquake had freed him from the constant pall of victimhood, and even the nagging desire for revenge. Were his parents' murderers evil? Beyond a doubt. But they unwittingly played into a chain of events that left Alden alive and enlightened. They'd been pawns in the machinations of the universe. And here now was Alden, emancipated.

His feelings about the bridge suddenly shifted from woeful futility to optimistic determination. He was not fighting a losing battle as an insignificant anomaly in the scheme of the cosmos. Alden was fulfilling a purpose. He didn't die with his parents and he didn't die in the earthquake. After all that, he wasn't going to answer those conditions by dying through surrender. Giving up would be the real crime.

Alden took a few steps to Burly and gave him a head hug.

"Burly," he said, "it's you and me, boy. We've got this. Let's build a bridge and get outa here."

Burly groaned softly.

"Yeah, I love you, too, Burly Boy." Alden stepped back over to the edge of the old cave hole. "Now, let's figure this out."

Alden climbed down in and stood on the collapsed slabs of stone.

"Hey, you know what, boy? I think we just got ourselves some more tree squishers here. We can haul these out and mash two at once. Think so?"

Sometimes Burly grunted at questions like this, other times he let them drift away rhetorically. He stayed silent. Maybe he was just not looking forward to dragging rocks again. Alden turned back to the ladder and started climbing out.

"We can get a couple of metal bars down in there and slide those rocks out on rails just like we did to get 'em onto the tree. Piece of cake. But first things first. I got no shelter now, Burly. Gonna have to build something. And all the corn needs to be rounded up. Corn on the cob. I know how you love that treat."

Even before those things, though, the very top of the list was getting the rocks at the flattening station back on the tree trunk there. The earthquake had shaken them off the tree, and it was only a few days away from being dry and ready. If they didn't get the weight back on it, they might be throwing away a month of processing time, and in Alden's refreshed frame of mind, that was completely unacceptable. After a few hours, they had the rocks righted and the tree under their pressure again. Then, Alden could afford to think about getting a roof over his head.

Alden knew right away how he was going to construct a shelter for himself. It was the perfect thing to do with all the remaining cinder blocks around the house foundation. His cave was in a fixed location, but his new home could be anywhere, and Alden could take the opportunity to cut way down on travel. The vast majority of trips were between the woods and the bridge, so just outside the garden would be good. It was going to be terrific to be able to finish working and not have to walk that last quarter mile out to the cave every evening, to say nothing of not going up and down the ladder every time. Alden realized he could actually have done this long ago, but his brain just didn't go there. It was fixed on the cave being home. Just another way that this new situation was liberating his thought processes.

It took most of the next day, but Alden and Burly got all the house cinder blocks up from the foundation and hauled to the edge of the garden. The roof was best made from flat planks of squashed brushtop, and as much as Alden hated to sacrifice any that used to be built into the bridge, shelter took priority. They started the long salvage process by hoisting roof planks up from the piles of wreckage in the ravine.

Alden had some clever fun designing his new shelter. He couldn't get extravagant with only two hundred cinder blocks, but he did make two simple rooms with a doorway between. Each room was just under eight feet wide and twelve long, the width designed to allow the planks to rest on top of the walls. The doorway was thirty inches, narrow enough so a plank could rest easily over it without falling in. One room was for Alden's sitting and sleeping logs, and the other was for anything else. It didn't accommodate Burly's full body length, but it could give him respite from the elements sometimes, or it could store crops or whatever else might come up. The fire pit was reconstructed a handy but safe distance from the entrance. It took three days to finish, but when he did, Alden was quite happy with it all and excited about living closer to the forest.

Next up would have been harvesting the corn, but Alden was having second thoughts about that effort. All the stalks were razed by the fierce winds, and that made a first impression on Alden's mind that he should hurry and gather everything. The ears weren't quite fully matured, but close, and plenty close enough to enjoy eating. The more Alden considered it, the more he was thinking there was probably no benefit to having the corn sitting in the second room of the shelter as opposed to staying on the stalks until they were going to be eaten. If there was a chance for the corn to keep getting any nourishment from the stalks and continue maturing, that was better. There were nearly a hundred plants, spaced well apart, and they were producing two harvestable ears per stalk, so that would mean quite a pile of plucked ears getting worse in storage instead of possibly still getting better on the stalk. He decided to start eating them but leave the rest alone.

Alden made another major decision about the garden. When he and Burly were rolling trees out of the way to make a path into the forest, he confirmed that the water pipeline from the pump to the garden was destroyed, crushed in numerous places by falling trees. Carrying enough water to the garden in his pot was out of the question, and they were already living almost exclusively off of fruitleaves, so Alden was faced with the idea that the garden would best be abandoned for now. He had carrot seeds and melon seeds, and both of those could be saved until the rainy season, now five months away. He'd plant those and let the rain give him natural rounds of crops, but that would have to be all he could plan on. By his calculations, he was about a year from completing the bridge, if he could flatten two trees at once, so one more round of carrot and melon treats next summer should be all they needed, anyway. Any time not spent on gardening was time building the bridge, which would speed that up all the more.

Next was getting a second station for flattening brushtops. There were hundreds of them sitting around drying, and they needed to get one under more rocks as quickly as possible. Alden's idea of using metal rails to get chunks of the collapsed cave roof up and out worked admirably. There was a problem, though. The cave wasn't as large as Alden first thought, and even with all the workable slabs hauled out, he only had enough to flatten perhaps half the length of a brushtop. They could get more rocks from very far away, but Alden could already tell that Burly was less energetic with this round of rocks than the first time. He was worried that he could really wear out his friend, and they both needed to make it all the way through this. If either of them ran out of steam, they were both sunk.

By the time they had the new rocks in place to begin squishing an extra half-brushtop, the trees felled by the earthquake were six days old, but Alden had to hope that in a month-long drying cycle, there was enough moisture left in the trunks to still let them flatten properly. The tree at the first station was complete and still nicely flat despite the interruption from the earthquake, so they were able to get two new trees started.

With all the large rocks excavated from his former cave, Alden was able to retrieve his stuff that was buried in there. There really wasn't anything to get damaged— just clothes, books, and a few small tools. It wasn't difficult to bring those up and get the dust washed out, and soon his new shelter had everything his old one did. With Burly's help, he even got his old log pulled out with the calendar notches on it, so he could keep going with that. He could have continued it on a new log, but seeing all the notches was a reminder of how far they'd come, even if just now they were practically back to square one.

With the most immediate recovery activities completed, it was time to make a new working plan. The impact of the quake event remained a little overwhelming, but Alden was focused on progress now, and to him that meant embracing his father's guidance about handling huge problems. Just figure out the next step. Decide what that is, and take that step. Every problem can be overcome, one piece at a time. Alden had already proven that to himself with all he and Burly had accomplished, and it remained true even in the face of being thrown back so many steps. It was still just as possible to tackle any situation. All he needed was the next task, then the next.

Besides the brushtop trunks, all the vines from the wind-blown trees were drying now, too, and Alden spent the next few days braiding rope while it was still easy to do. Apart from being the next logical step, it gave Burly some rest after moving so many rocks.

Alden felt sorry for him, but Burly seemed to share his determination. Working together had a renewed sense of both urgency and camaraderie, and Alden had never been so satisfied to have his companion with him through this entire fantastical circumstance. Unique situations create unique outcomes, and regardless of the tragic basis for their mutual dependence, the two of them were family.

One of Alden's favorite aspects of sharing life with Burly was their evenings. Alden was good at knowing when the sun was still just high enough to be able to start a fire, and although they usually didn't have anything to cook, campfire time was their opportunity to relax. It kept the days from feeling like nothing but work from sunup to sundown. Sometimes Alden would feel chatty and talk to Burly all evening; sometimes they just watched the fire. Alden sang songs from time to time, and that seemed to touch something in Burly, who would groan softly to join in the sound, almost as if he were humming. It happened most often when Alden sang "Edelweiss," a song he knew because his father sometimes sang it to his mother. It wasn't really a love song, but it sounded like one when Dad sang it.

Alden didn't stay up into the blackness of night very often. For one, he was usually tired, and getting sleep was important. For another, he was diligently wary of having an unnatural campfire possibly draw the attention of the predatory birds. Not long after the new shelter was built, though, were two nights of double full moons, and that was not to be missed. It only happened every eight months, and Alden indulged in the hope that they may only be around on the plateau to see one more.

With lots of new rope available, it was time to begin the arduous task of salvaging everything in the ravine and reconstructing the bridge. It was more difficult to stand trees up from the ravine into the right spot than to tip them over the edge, but there were too many of them dried and ready. They couldn't lose the time waiting a month for the brushtops in the forest to harden. The old ropes were mostly a loss; they were nice and strong, but they were brittle and couldn't be untied as easily as using the newer ropes Alden just braided. He found his hanging ladder in one piece, which was helpful. One less thing to build again; one small contributor to Alden's optimism as they plunged into this monumental effort once again.

Chapter 23

Considering it had taken six months to get where they'd been with those first forty feet of bridge, taking only two more to put those pieces back in place was quite a victory. In that time, two rounds of new plank squishing were also complete. With more dried, round tree trunks than they would ever need already available, Alden knew plank production would still be the limiting factor in their schedule, but at least they had increased that from what it was earlier.

It was rigorous, exhausting work. All day, every day. Up and down ladders, hauling trees, sharpening the hatchet and machete, pulling and tying vine ropes. Sometimes one would break, and a bracing tree would plummet into the ravine. Through it all, there was washing and carrying fresh pots of water and trips into the forest for drinking and fruitleaves. It was arduous and repetitive in many ways, and the crushed water pipeline meant they couldn't play in the gushing flow from the irrigation tube anymore, but Burly still sometimes galloped across the open rock, allowing Alden to indulge in the exhilaration.

Fruitleaves tended not to last very long after they were plucked. Alden tried boiling some once, too. Fresh was better. It was weeks since the last of their corn was gone, and months ahead with nothing to eat but fruitleaves.

Besides the monotony, Alden was worried about his nutrition. He was a growing boy getting ridiculous amounts of exercise, yet he didn't feel quite as strong, sturdy, and alert as he used to. He sensed that his body was not really developing properly on a fruitleaf diet, and it was critical to maintain health and strength. The bridge was almost halfway complete, which was tremendous, but Alden couldn't risk a declining physical condition putting anything in jeopardy down the stretch. He had to make a creative decision.

Alden eventually settled on the only option he could think of for food—birds. He had some planning and preparations to make, and he knew it would devote two days of their time just to go get some, but it was the right thing to do. It was an unavoidable reality.

Part of the preparations was considering walking in the bird habitat. The poop was omnipresent, and he had no intention of sacrificing his only shoes to that effort. Although he could wash his feet if he went barefoot, that was risky for other reasons. If the bird poop was hiding a sharp bit of tree bark or something, he might cut himself and get immediately infected. Thinking about tree bark gave him an idea, and he fashioned some crude foot coverings out of the purple-grey bark of the brushtops. They were simple, rolled tubes of bark tied around his foot and ankle with vine rope. It was less than comfortable, but would only need to be in place for a short time.

As thick as the birds were, Alden figured he didn't need to get really fancy about how to trap or hunt them. He was planning to take a chunk of brushtop wood about the length of a broom handle, and trust that if he stood in the melee of birds and swung it around a while he couldn't help but hit some.

Alden chose a morning, and he and Burly headed out to the bird habitat. By early afternoon, they were standing within the last of the brushtops at the edge of the bird woods where they had been before, marveling at the aviary amid the tremendous noise and stench. This whole thing suddenly seemed like a long shot to Alden, but he slid down off of Burly, removed his shoes and socks, and tied his bark slippers in place. With his brushtop club in hand, he took a deep breath.

"Well, here goes nothin', Burly," he said loudly over the din of the birds. "Wish me luck."

He trudged out into the bird trees. The smell was horrifying, and Alden had to use high steps to make sure he didn't scoop up poop with his feet. Birds whizzed by, making Alden flinch and raise his elbow to protect his face several times. He chose a spot in the middle of four trees, took the club in both hands, and waved it quickly in an arc directly over his head.

Astoundingly, he struck a bird. It was a redhead, and Alden was thrilled with his immediate success as it zoomed on a line to the ground twenty feet away, then dismayed as he watched it bounce and roll and become completely covered in bird droppings. It was only then that he realized he had swung in a direction away from where Burly was standing on clean ground within the nearby brushtops, and that it might actually be possible to swat birds into the forest near Burly if he swung that direction. The border of the poop domain was only slightly farther that direction than where the batted redhead landed the opposite way.

Disorienting, deafening, and disodorous though it was, Alden was smiling at what he now viewed more as a sport. He turned his body around so it was easy to use the club over his head in Burly's direction, and let loose with a mighty swing.

Nothing. All air.

He tried again. Another whiff.

Once more, he came up empty, but on the next attempt he landed a blow on a blue bird and watched it sail on an arc and land a few feet away from Burly's right hind leg.

Alden yelled out with delight. "Wa-hoo! Ya see that, Burly?"

Burly stood motionless, with a look in his eye. Often, Alden wasn't sure exactly what was going on in Burly's head, but sometimes the look was clear. This time the unmistakable message was to whack some birds so they could go home.

"Killjoy," said Alden.

He kept swinging, with what he considered surprising results. It only took twenty swings to hit six birds. Six he could use. He actually hit seven, but one went off sideways into the poop.

Alden had made a game of it and was having as much fun as he might under the circumstances, but he did feel bad about killing birds, especially the ones he couldn't take with him. To Alden, though, this had become a matter of survival, and all bets were off in that game, including some small collateral damage. He stopped when he had as many as he wanted to try to work with this first time, so he didn't feel like he was being wasteful, but hunting for food was necessary and could have unfortunate consequences. He didn't feel obligated to try to clean all the poop off the two birds that landed poorly, and nobody could make him. Eating the birds was enough of a disease risk without introducing a grossly unsanitary cleaning operation. As much as he appreciated his place in nature, he also sometimes felt like this was his life and—for the time being—his forest, and if he pulled off a stunt like building a bridge across the ravine, karma would just have to spot him a couple extra dead birds.

With a half-dozen prizes wrapped in a shirt in his pouch, Alden and Burly headed back. They did have to pick a place to sleep during the night hours, but tried to keep it short, and by mid-morning the next day they were arriving back at the shelter.

Alden chose a place out in the rocky terrain that was well away from their normal pathways, and began the task of figuring out how to get any meat out of the birds. He had four blues and two redheads. The blues were reasonably substantial, like a raven; the redheads more of a robin's size. Early in his salvaging searches, Alden had found some silverware, and it included two steak knives. He'd had no call for something that small or flimsy up to now, but here he was with the perfect chance to use one. It was pretty disgusting to cut into a dead bird, but Alden tried to move quickly and keep convincing himself it was to get survival protein.

He knew better than to try to pluck the feathers. There was no way that would be worth the effort. The first bird took the longest, because that one was basically an anatomy lesson. He sliced the skin down the breast and stomach, then tried to peel it away to the left and right. That was difficult and messy, and eventually required more cuts, but when he revealed the bird's innards he saw what he thought he might. Nothing but guts from the breastbone down, and only two chunks of meat worth dealing with in the upper body. Besides the unwieldy nature of the machete blade, it was otherwise fairly obvious how to cut the breast meat pieces out.

They were actually larger than he was expecting, too—about the size of a chicken egg.

The second bird was a little faster, since Alden knew what he was after, but it wasn't until the fourth one that he tried a different type of cut, across the middle of the bird so he could pull the skin up instead of separating it left and right. That was the best way. With eight blue bird breasts and four smaller ones from the redheads, he was intrigued by the size of his meal. If they were good to eat and didn't make him sick, he could do this as often as he needed to, and that was extremely encouraging.

Alden took everything down to the stream with his pot and got it all washed up, then went straight to cooking. He didn't really have any way other than boiling at the moment, but that got the job done. It was tough, and had a strong taste that clearly needed salt and pepper, but it was palatable, made all the better by simply not being a fruitleaf.

This all took until late afternoon, and Alden thought it best if he just let his digestion work on the meat for the rest of the day. That was smart, as he did go through some discomfort, but by evening it was smoothing out.

His hunting expedition was a success, and that gave him tremendous confidence. He didn't relish the thought of giving up two days for every meal of meat, but the trade-off was being healthier and maintaining the strength to complete the bridge in the first place, so whatever it took would have to be acceptable. Soon, he'd be in a position of waiting for trees to flatten, anyway, so bird swatting wouldn't really be prolonging the schedule. The upshot was that Alden had figured out how to conquer yet another obstacle in his path, and that felt very, very good.

◄❖►

When the rainy season hit, Alden and Burly had roughly eighty feet of the bridge built. Seeing the far side of the ravine just that much closer was a great feeling. Progress was in small chunks, but every tree or plank they moved out to the end was hauled across a combined eighty feet of that progress, and that was a motivator. The rain was not.

Living in the house with Mom and Dad, it was easy not to pay close attention to just how heavy and persistent the rains were, and they slowed Alden down more than he was planning. He didn't think getting wet would change the operation much, but it made everything slicker and more difficult to handle. It also virtually halted the tree flattening; they weren't drying out at all. Some days the deluge was so depressingly constant Alden just sat in his shelter, with Burly lying in the second room. Those days were interminable, but Alden seemed to sense it was part of Burly's natural cycle to be less active that time of year, and he didn't push it. It was not easy, but Alden convinced himself to accept that fighting nature could invite more problems than working with it.

There was one thing Alden did think to prepare for—no fires. Without refrigeration, he couldn't stock up on bird meat, but he made sure he ate lots of it during the last sunny month. He never invested the time to see if there were any plants on the plateau that could be used as seasonings, but he did whittle himself some skewer sticks that would allow him to cook directly over the flame, and that gave him some variety. The best part was that the protein intake had the desired effect on his physical development. He felt great, with muscles that were toning differently than they ever had. It was well worth the periodic outings into the bird poop.

Alden had also remembered to prepare for the rains by planting his carrots and melons. The slower pace made him all the more grateful for that, as he was now certain they'd be building long enough for the crops to come in, perhaps more than once. He held back some of the carrot seeds in case they were still on the plateau through another rain cycle, and he was a little worried they wouldn't stay viable for that long, since he'd harvested all of them. Nothing to do about that now, except maybe try to grow more plants to seed, but carrots were too big a treat now, for both he and Burly. If they had plants, they were going to eat them.

After all the struggles and trials Alden had overcome, it struck him as odd that one of the most frustrating obstacles he'd encountered was just plain waiting. There were no problem-solving techniques for the rain. Alden was forced to add patience to the list of lessons on the plateau.

Chapter 24

It was two months after the end of the rain; one month since Alden turned twelve. He'd grown some more, and noticed it most in his hands and feet. He still had to use extra socks for the foot in Dad's shoe, but Mom's fit without that now.

He had three shirts from his father. One had long sleeves—the one he'd used as a bandage. The sleeves were long for him yet, and in the daily sun it wasn't very comfortable; between that and all the blood stains, he left that one for potential bandage use. There were two with short sleeves, though; one light green with buttons, the other a white polo shirt. Alden wore the white one, mostly, and now used his dad's tan cargo shorts held up by vine suspenders. From the safari hat down to his right shoe, he was in his father's wardrobe now, and that helped keep him always close to his parents' memory.

Burly was older, too. Alden hadn't any idea how long burlons lived, but he had the sense to recognize that Burly was on the downhill side. He never wavered in their daily activities, but everything required a touch more time and effort than it used to. When Alden showed his affection for Burly with a pat or rub on the snout—something he did often—he began to notice that the hairs around Burly's mouth, where they were once thin and light, were now thicker, more coarse, and completely white. There were also light gray spots forming around Burly's nostrils and eyes. They didn't look sickly or dangerous; they seemed to just be signs of aging, but aging Burly was.

The bridge was a hundred feet long now. Half the task. There'd clearly been setbacks, but they were actually more or less on the schedule Alden had laid out a year earlier. As the grassland grew ever closer, practically taunting Alden with its grainy fragrances, he was thinking more and more about what lay ahead. What in the world would become of him and Burly? Burly had a family over there. Every so often, he trumpeted his mournful call to them, and they answered. They never came within sight, which Alden thought was odd, but in a way he was thankful for that. If Dad or Mom were standing on the edge of the grassland, it would be very hard to pull away and get any work done, and Alden didn't want Burly to go through the pain of tearing himself away from the presence of his family just so he could work with Alden.

Once the bridge was finished, though, Burly would go to be with them, as he should. But what would that mean for Alden? If the Grass Camp was completely destroyed the way his house was, and there was no escape for him off that planet, he would want to stay with Burly. Would he be welcome with the burlons? Would Burly even treat him the same? Would he be able to live in the grassland?

Many thoughts and possible scenarios for Alden's future floated through his mind, and one was the twisted notion that he might actually need to come back to the plateau to live. Live in the land he knew, with food and water he was familiar with, and his shelter. There were dangers in the grassland. Poisonous crabs, hairless cats, and huge demons with black feathers.

Or perhaps there were supplies at the Grass Camp that would help him live and hunt. Maybe crab meat and cat meat were delicious. There were so, so many questions to answer.

Regardless of the life waiting for Alden, there was only one way to discover his future. Finish the bridge.

There was only thirty feet to go. Thirty feet of air between the last plank of the bridge and the firm, safe edge of the grassland. The anticipation of stepping on that edge was palpable.

With the nearer vantage point, Alden was beginning to adjust height and direction to make sure the bridge level ended up where it should. Although the grassland had topsoil the rocky portion of the plateau did not share, the edge right at the ravine was primarily rock, left more barren by the buggy trail leading up to the bridge. The ravine wall was essentially vertical, but within a few feet of the top it angled slightly out of the ravine. On Alden's side, the ravine edges were fairly pronounced, but over in the grassland the top foot or so created a more gently curved lip.

It was a long time to get within thirty feet. Almost another year. They weren't building at their earlier pace. Everything was slower, mostly because Burly had to rest more. Each tree that got chopped down for flattening into planks came from slightly deeper in the forest, hauled out past all of the long-hardened tree trunks from the earthquake.

The big earthquake, that is. There were two more since then, but neither one did much damage. One snapped the joint on a bracing tree in the bridge frame, but that wasn't difficult to fix, and the bridge didn't seem noticeably wobblier from either quake. Alden had no way to know if the bridge had actually gotten weaker, so there was no choice but to act as though it hadn't.

Sliding the squishing rocks onto the fresh trees for flattening was the hardest thing for Burly, but that only came once a month. Perhaps because of that, it was easier for Alden to see a difference from month to month in how difficult it was. But Burly never faltered in determination or attitude. Alden knew Burly could feel the closeness of the goal every bit as much as Alden did. For all the loss and hardship, Alden simply could not conceive of a life in which he was not brothers with this magnificent, astounding companion. They had joined souls.

With regular bird protein in his diet, Alden had grown normally over the year, which is to say a lot. His right foot was fine in his dad's shoe, but his left could no longer tolerate his mom's. Alden fashioned a more permanent version of a bark slipper, tailored better and made to stay on more firmly through his work. With a couple pairs of socks for comfort, it was functional and tolerable.

Alden awoke and checked his notch calendar. He knew precision wasn't exact after all that had transpired, but by his estimation, it was his thirteenth birthday. He and Burly would have to do something special. It was a month after the rain, and their new carrot crop was young, but they might just have to steal a few.

He stepped out of the shelter into the morning sun. These days, it was odd not to see Burly right nearby.

Alden never knew what, if anything, Burly did after Alden was asleep, but it was obvious Burly was keenly in touch with Alden's patterns. Burly was always standing around waiting for the day as soon as Alden was good to go. Today, no Burly.

Within seconds, a bolt of fear shot down Alden's spine as he looked out into the forest area and saw Burly lying down. They'd used many of the nearby tree trunks for bridge posts and braces, and with those out of the way, Alden clearly saw Burly a few hundred feet past the garden. He could have just been resting longer that day and a little off on his timing, but that's not how it struck Alden.

"Burly!" Alden yelled as he sprinted through the garden toward his friend. He screamed it again as he got close and skidded up near Burly's head on his knees. Burly was on his left side. His eyes were closed. Alden had never seen Burly's eyes closed. Not for longer than a blink. Those wonderfully expressive, comforting, knowing eyes were shut.

Alden quickly noticed that Burly's belly was moving with breaths, so he was alive, but this was not good. He laid a hand on the side of Burly's head.

"Burly! Come on, boy!"

There was a strange, yellow foam around Burly's mouth and nostrils, and some on the ground beneath his snout. Alden put an ear down close and could hear a frightening raspiness to Burly's breathing. It was never smooth, but what Alden heard now was a disturbing gurgle from deep inside. Burly was very, very ill.

Alden began to cry. He was deeply panicked at the shocking thought of what could be happening. In all the ways Alden's life played out in his head, losing Burly before he got home was never there. He knew intellectually that Burly was older and weaker than he used to be, but actually considering Burly might not make it to the grassland was unfathomable. It was utterly beyond conception, as far from his imagining as that horrible, fateful day when he turned eleven.

"Wake up, boy!"

He stroked Burly's jowl gently. The thick, leathery, grey-brown skin never felt so soft.

"Wake up, please."

Alden couldn't dream of dealing with this. If Burly died, there would be no coping. He wanted to just take his machete and rip his own heart out.

"Let's go, Burly. Time to get started." Alden's voice cracked between heavy sobs.

"You can do it, boy. You can. Just ... open your eyes and look at me."

As he had done a thousand times before, Burly responded as if he knew every word. His wrinkled eyelids parted slowly, then blinked twice, then opened. Alden had never been so thrilled to look into the huge, brown eyes of his beloved friend.

"Burly!" Despite the situation, Alden laughed through his tears.

"Burly! I'm here, Burly Boy! What do you need? I can get you anything you need. We even have carrots, now, boy. I can get you carrots."

Burly lifted his head slightly. Alden was nothing but nervous energy.

"Oh, careful. How are you feeling? Wow, that's a stupid question. You're sick, aren't you. We can fix that. I don't know how, but we can do it. We can make you better."

Burly raised his legs the way he did to get his weight leveraged so he could lower them and roll to his feet. Alden stood to get out of the way.

"Careful, boy."

Burly stood. His head was low, and he wheezed several globs of yellow foam out onto the ground.

"That's it, boy. Get that stuff out of you. Must be some kind of infection."

Seemingly ignoring Alden, Burly turned and began walking slowly out toward the flattening station for full-length trees.

"Wait a minute, boy," said Alden as he rushed up alongside. "Are you OK? What're you doin'?"

Burly grunted slightly, sounding like he was under water.

"OK, OK, you don't have to answer me. But shouldn't you rest? Oh, right, don't answer. I guess you know best. I'll go along, if this is what you want to do."

Burly was lethargic, but he didn't stop until he was at the flat tree. Without hesitation, he leaned his body forward, put a foot up on one of the rocks, and shoved it off.

"Whoa, boy! That's not how we do this."

That was true. They typically got a rope harness attached to Burly and pulled each rock away. That was less stress on Burly, but this was much faster. With determination, and sometimes hacking up yellow phlegm in between, Burly went one by one down the tree and shoved all the rocks. Then he stood at one end and tossed his head in the air toward the ravine.

"Are you sure, boy? You want to do this now?"

By this time, Alden knew very well what Burly was doing and why. Alden was a complete mess of emotions, wanting to appreciate this time and aching to explode with grief in the realization that Burly knew he was not going to get better.

With Burly's clear signal that he wanted to drag the tree, Alden knew what he had to do, and it sickened him to understand they were desperate to do it while Burly was alive.

It was only fitting that Burly made the last design decision on the bridge, and that is exactly what he had effectively done. There was only a gap of thirty feet between the bridge and the grassland. Dragging the flat tree whole, without chopping it in thirds first, meant they were going to try to set it directly across the entire gap as a single plank. The flat tree was plenty long enough; it was one of the longest they'd chopped, at almost forty-five feet, but they couldn't stand it and tip it down over the gap. They would have to shove it into place fast enough that it caught the far edge before it tipped into the ravine. The larger, heavier end would be on the bridge, but thirty feet was too much more than half the tree length for it to not tip into the ravine if they weren't quick enough.

They had another tree that was half flat, but there was no margin for error. They had to do this one right. A single plank wasn't wide enough for Burly, so if either plank didn't set in place properly, Burly would not be able to cross. Alden wasn't ready to think about how to get the second tree set in place. It was shorter, and the small end was round, and they would have to set both planks so the smaller ends were together on the edge of the grassland. It would have to work absolutely perfectly for Burly to be able to cross. It was too much to keep thinking about right now. First things first. Besides, it was going to be enough of a miracle to get the first one in place.

"All right, boy, let's do it," said Alden. "Let me get my things." He ran into the shelter and grabbed his safari hat and pouch, then returned to get Burly harnessed to the tree.

The trip to the ravine was laborious for Burly and emotionally tumultuous for Alden. He chatted as close to normally as he could, mostly out of an odd sense that fussing over Burly too much was somehow inappropriate. Burly was obviously sick and hurting but manning up for this task, and out of respect for that,

Alden felt he needed to do the same.

Discovering Burly on the forest floor had really felt much like discovering his parents, and the unspeakable pain of that was more than Alden could consider bearing. But now was a reprieve he hadn't gotten before. Now was a brief chance to share and appreciate time wrapped in the finality of knowing they would soon not be together. Time to say goodbye. And in the similarity between the two astonishing losses, Alden was actually saying goodbye to Mom and Dad as well.

Burly was weak. It seemed he had even gotten noticeably more frail on the way to the bridge. Alden kept his energy up and spoke of Burly getting to rest soon to regain his strength before they brought the second tree, then of going home. Of finally reaching the promised land of grass.

They got as close to the end of the bridge as they could with dragging. Now it was time to push the tree plank in place, and they repositioned Burly behind the end of it.

"Are you ready for this?" said Alden. "We can rest first. I know you're awfully tired."

Burly tossed his head, then lowered it to get in position on the trunk. Alden put a hand on his head.

"Wait."

Burly looked up.

"You have to do this one fast, OK?" Alden lowered his head and ran a couple of steps. "Fast."

Burly nodded, for the first time without the slightest hint of the characteristic ambiguity in his motions Alden had learned to interpret over their time together. Alden stepped back to him and put his arms around the back of his head. He held them there a moment, smelling Burly's rough, earthy skin.

"I love you, Burly. I love you, boy. Thank you."

Burly grunted.

Alden released his hug and moved away down the

plank, in case there was anything he could do to help guide it or something. Burly coughed up some yellow gunk, then put his head down again to get ready. He hadn't pushed a flat plank before; only round tree trunks. It was difficult to get enough of his head on the end of the tree, but in a moment he found it and was ready to go.

Chapter 25

Burly leaned into the plank log and began pushing. Within a couple of steps he made a small groan and accelerated strongly. The tree slid swiftly down the remaining few feet of the bridge deck, and Alden ran next to it, looking down at it to see if it kept going straight.

Alden pulled up at the edge of the bridge as the plank sped out over the opening. With clenched hands and nerves, Alden held his breath as the leading end neared the rock face of the grassland, then began to tip down. It struck the ravine wall a couple feet below the lip.

There was just enough angle in the rock wall to propel the plank upward from the impact of Burly's force. Alden watched intently as it bowed slightly, splintered a little, and sprang wiggling into the air like an overstressed diving board, then bounced twice and came to rest with the tip just catching the gently curved edge of the ravine.

Alden was silent for a moment as he stared at the far end of the plank to see if was going to stay in place. Satisfied that it would, he thrust his arms into the air.

"Wa-hoo! You did it, Burly!" He turned to congratulate his amazing buddy. "We have a—"

Alden stopped at the sight of Burly. The first time he saw Burly lying down today, he was driven by the instinct to run to him. This time, he was petrified to go near him.

"Burly?"

Alden took a step, then moved more quickly to him. Burly was on his left side again, and Alden ran around him to kneel at his face as he did before. There was an air of inevitability in Alden's voice as he spoke again.

"Burly? Are you there, boy?"

There was more yellow foam around Burly's mouth and nostrils, and Alden put his ear down close to listen again. Nothing but the gentle wafting of the breeze through the tall blades of grass not far away.

Alden gazed up at Burly's belly, looking for some sign of rhythmic movement in his hulking body. There was none. Alden began to weep as he crawled over and rested his ear just behind Burly's shoulder, hoping beyond hope to hear something. Heartbeat, wheezing, anything.

It was silent.

Alden turned and collapsed to the ground, sitting with his legs out in front of him, the back of his head resting in the crook between Burly's leg and chest. He closed his eyes and cried, but not like before. This somehow stunned him in a way that was different from pure emotional pain. This was more like Burly was a vital lobe of Alden's brain, and someone reached in and ripped it out.

After all they had done, and all the promises Alden made to get Burly home, it was Burly who gave every last ounce of his life to get Alden across the ravine.

Alden opened his eyes and stared at the cloudless sky. The day was a day like any other day. The stream was still coursing through the ravine beneath him. The birds in the forest were still flitting away in their frenetic chaos. Everything was the same, but everything was catastrophically not the same. What nerve had the universe to blithely continue in the face of this event. Without the slightest pause to honor this magnificent beast, this deepest friend and companion who had showed Alden more of the best ways to be human than most humans he'd met.

He could go now. He could leave the plateau, yet now there was no reason. It served no purpose to continue. There was nothing to accomplish that would not be dwarfed by his failure to complete the only task he'd had for two years. Get Burly home.

Alden remained motionless for some time. Most of an hour. His mind swirled around many thoughts of what to do next, including absolutely nothing. Many feelings and ideas flowed through his mind until he entertained the notion that if the universe owed Burly a tribute, certainly he did, and the only way to honor Burly's memory was to step into the grassland and continue the life Burly made possible. Once that idea crept in, it nagged at Alden more and more until he knew that feeling sorry for himself was a luxurious disgrace. Wherever Burly was, he would rightly be ashamed of Alden if this heroic effort went unfulfilled.

The decision was made, and with it came the familiar determination that drove Alden to this point. He would get to the Grass Camp and find something there, some way to make this all matter. To make it somehow reflect a fraction of the sacrifice Burly made. In his mind, that was his new promise to Burly.

That meant it was time to leave. Time to actually get up and walk away from his buddy. It had to happen, but there was one thing first.

Before he moved, before he even lifted an arm, he took a deep breath and softly sang "Edelweiss."

Alden's joints were a little stiff as he stood up, and he felt somewhat spent from the trauma. This was no longer a time for dwelling, though. It was time to move ahead, and show both Burly and his parents that he would charge headlong into the next adventure. His pouch already had everything he figured to want with him: hatchet, water, a couple day-old fruitleaves, bird talon, and his microscope eyepiece lens for fires. The machete was already on the bridge, and he picked it up, adjusted the safari hat on his head, and looked around again.

He stood briefly in final acknowledgement of not only Burly but everything that transpired over their many months together.

"Goodbye, Burly Boy. Thanks for being my friend."

Alden turned and took a few steps back toward the plateau, looking down into the ravine at the wreckage of the camp buggy.

"Goodbye, Mom and Dad. Thanks for loving me and making me miss you so much." Tears came to his eyes again. "I miss you so much."

He let out a sigh, then started away. First was walking around Burly again, and when he did, he noticed that the near end of the final plank was buried beneath his back. In that first moment when the plank landed on the far edge of the ravine, Alden was elated but concerned that putting weight on it would make it slip right down into the ravine. With Burly holding it down, there was no chance of that. It would stay sturdy. There wasn't the slightest doubt in Alden's mind that Burly had done that on purpose. Even as he passed away, Burly, incredibly, made sure Alden could get across.

"You are truly amazing, boy," said Alden as he got down on his hands and knees. The plank was thirty inches wide, plenty of room for walking, but it would get narrower as he went, and Alden wasn't about to risk anything like a gust of breeze ruining this moment.

He crawled steadily across the plank, which held firmly in place. At the far end, Alden reached out with a hand and touched the ground, then finished his careful crawling off the plank. Still on his hands and knees, he leaned down and kissed the dirt. He stood and took a few steps forward until he was comfortably present in the grassland, then smiled broadly and put his hands on his hips as he surveyed his new surroundings.

Alden wanted to let out a triumphant yell, but thought better of it. Except for one twisted bird, the plateau was a quarantined domain. Here in the grassland, even though he was but a few feet from the bridge, it suddenly felt like yelling could call undue attention to himself.

Despite the time already gone, Alden estimated he could still get to the Grass Camp during that day's sunlight. It was fifty miles away, and with a brisk combination of walking and jogging he could cover that in eight hours or less. Fortunately, fitness and stamina were not an issue with Alden. The sun was still not at its peak, so if nothing slowed him down he'd arrive with a couple hours of daylight to look around.

Alden stopped for water and a snack a few times, but stuck to his plan and kept moving swiftly. He really didn't want to get stuck in the grassland overnight. He remembered the story told by Randy from the Grass Camp about two weeks of fever from being pinched by one of the local crabs. Alden could possibly find his way to a tree to climb for sleeping, but had no idea what else could climb, like a hairless cat. It had him spooked thoroughly enough to keep him on the move at a brisk pace, jogging whenever he could persist and walking when he couldn't. The only question was whether the Grass Camp could help with any shelter or protection when he arrived.

It felt strange to be doing something without Burly. It harkened back to the first couple of days after his parents were killed, when he was completely on his own. That seemed like a lifetime ago. As he traveled, Alden thought some more about both his parents and Burly, weaving back and forth between feeling privileged that he ever knew them and abandoned through losing everyone he ever loved. But he kept fighting to find that thread of commitment to all of them that he would honor their memories by living as they would have helped him to live. He kept moving along quickly toward the Grass Camp.

Fortunately, there was no navigation required to get to his destination. The buggy path was clear; there were two years of small plants creeping in, but the wheel lanes were still just dirt. It provided unobstructed passage to the camp.

The first happy thing Alden noticed when he got near was that he could see buildings. That immediately meant the destruction was not as thorough as it was at his house.

"Hey!" Alden said as soon as he thought he might be in earshot of survivors. Having people hear him was way more important than trying not to announce his location to animals.

"Hello!"

Not surprisingly, there was no response of any kind. Alden had long ago surmised there were no humans here, since they would have come checking on the situation at the plateau early on. Still, he couldn't help but toss out a lifeline in case something strange had occurred.

He came up to where the buggy path turned into the camp between two buildings, and rushed along to see anything he could.

"It's Alden! Hello!"

The camp was laid out in four buildings with the buggy path as a sort of short street between them, with two buildings on either side, spaced roughly twenty feet apart, front doors facing the buggy path. Straight ahead, just past the second pair of buildings, was a car port. It was nothing but a metal awning on four legs, and it had room under it for two buggies. One was back in the ravine.

The other was here, parked under the awning, and heavily damaged. It looked burned out. The awning itself had collapsed and was resting on top of the buggy, leaning down into the empty second stall. Whoever attacked his home had definitely been here.

Alden stopped near the center of the four buildings and called out a couple more times, but this place was clearly quiet and uninhabited. Looking around, he could see obvious damage. Each building had solar panels on the roof, and those had all been hit with some kind of weapon blast. The attackers disabled the power. They also dumped the water supply. The Grass Camp had no natural water close enough to pump like the Plateau Camp, so there was a small version of a water tower behind one of the barracks. That had been blasted and drained.

The barracks were the most damaged. The front corner of one was blasted away, allowing Alden to see inside, and the front door and windows of the other had been smashed away. The front door of the supply building was also missing. Alden did make note that there was no apparent earthquake damage here, meaning the intensity of the devastation was localized around the plateau. Just his luck.

All things considered, though, he realized the earthquake was a blessing in disguise. It allowed for a second flattening station, keeping the bridge construction schedule at least as short as it would have otherwise been. It prodded him to build his shelter, which was a considerable improvement. Perhaps most importantly, it liberated his attitude about losing his parents, considering what may have befallen them had none of this happened. Looking around the Grass Camp, though, he was freshly reminded that the crime was not only against him or his parents, and that was distressing. He knew from a distance that his friends, the other families on Cappa Terse, had been dealt a similar blow, but seeing it all in front of him made it very real and renewed some of the outrage that had found a dormant place beneath the surface of Alden's daily life. This was an infuriating injustice and a deeply saddening loss.

Alden began a search of each of the buildings, wary of what he might find but needing to know what was there. First was the barracks. That's what they were called, but they were much like Alden's house without the lab, since there was a separate building for that. Larger than his house, in fact, because there were more people in each. One had a family of four, and the other had two families of three. Alden chose the more damaged one, and climbed in through the hole in the corner.

Chapter 26

Things were messy. Alden went from room to room, finding disheveled evidence of frantic violence. It made him think about the terror his friends experienced there. With his house, everything was obliterated; here, it was easier to imagine what might have gone on while they were under attack. Were they slaughtered? Perhaps tortured and questioned? If so, about what? It was extremely disturbing.

Curiously, Alden was conscious to look for blood stains to help paint the picture of how the massacre unfolded, but he saw none. From that building, at least, it would seem they were herded outside to be executed. He was a little surprised at his own interest in even trying to recreate those moments in his mind. None of it truly mattered, and if anyone did make it out alive, ECOP would already have their account of what occurred. Imagining horrific events only served to torment Alden and revisit the day Mom and Dad were murdered. Even so, it was impossible to survey this scene without constructing the past. Alden had come to terms with the attackers regarding his parents. What happened at the Grass Camp, though, was refueling his anger.

The second barracks building was much like the first. Some ransacking and disarray, but no blood or bodies. The supply building was virtually empty. The attackers cleaned everything out, and that may have been why they didn't simply annihilate the buildings here as they did at Alden's house.

Last was the lab. Alden saved it for last on purpose, so he would know what condition everything else was in when he got what he expected to be bad news about the potential for communicating with ECOP. Instead, it was in the best shape of anywhere. There was evidence of some weapon blasts around the main room, but they looked like random vandalism, and that equipment was the environmental research stuff, not communications. The transmitter was in a smaller room adjacent to the main lab, and it seemed little or nothing was disturbed in there.

The huge question remained whether or not Alden could get power going. The solar panels would take lots of time and know-how to repair, but there would have been a back-up generator somewhere, just as there was at Alden's house. He went outside to look behind the buildings, and found the machine he was after, in back of the second barracks. That was the one on the same side of the buggy path as the lab, and Alden traced a thick cable running on the ground between the buildings. It was possible the emergency plan was to be able to keep one barracks and the lab building powered, and that was Alden's fervent hope.

There was a large, covered panel on the side of the generator, very similar to the one on the water pump near the spring pond on the plateau. Beneath the lid were some controls, including a scary-looking knife switch set to "Off." Beside that was a toggle switch with three positions, "Run," "Start," and "Off," which was also set to "Off." On top of it was a pull cord. Alden thought about what this all meant for a moment, then flipped the toggle to "Start" and pulled the cord.

It was very difficult the first time. He didn't get much of a yank on it. The second time was better, and he got it pulled all the way out, but nothing happened. For his third try, he put a foot on the side of the machine, grabbed the pull cord handle with both hands, and gave it a strong, fast heave. There was sputtering, then nothing. A sign of life.

On the fourth attempt, the generator coughed and popped a few times, then finally rumbled into a rhythmic churn. This was typically when he would have called to Burly and let out a victorious whoop, but Alden simply smiled and flipped the toggle to "Run." The generator continued churning.

Alden glanced around at the barracks and lab, but didn't see any evidence of power. He figured that was what the knife switch was for, but didn't want to flip it if he didn't have to. He grabbed the red, rubber tip of the switch and pushed it into the "On" position, and he could immediately see lights inside the barracks.

This was very, very exciting. Alden ran around to the front of the lab and darted inside. There was a lamp on one of the research desks that was burning brightly. He scooted into the communications room and sat at the desk of equipment.

There were several machines, but only one that mattered. Alden knew it well, the same model of transmitter they had on the plateau. It was still on. There were little red lights and an illuminated meter. There was the round grill on the front that protected the microphone and speaker, and the green button next to that reading, "Talk." Alden didn't know how to set things like frequency, but they only spoke to one place from here. ECOP. Flushed with prickly nerves, he cleared his throat and pushed the green button.

"Hello? Hello ECOP?"

He waited a moment.

"This is ECOP," a man's voice on the radio said. "Who is this?"

Alden nearly fainted off the chair. He had done it! He had survived. He and Burly had built a bridge. A bridge! A two-hundred-foot bridge across the ravine. And now here he was, the faint hope of everything they had done together coming alive on this desk before him. *He was speaking to ECOP.*

Alden took his finger off the button and looked up.

"Holy cannoli! We did it, Burly! We did it. I'm talkin' to ECOP, boy. Thanks, Burly Boy. We made it."

Alden pressed the button again, his voice wavering from the excitement.

"This ... this is Alden Waverly at the Grass Camp on Cappa Terse."

There was another moment of silence.

"Who are you?" the radio man said. "This is an ECOP protected frequency. Stop broadcasting and change your frequency immediately."

"No, no," said Alden. "It's me. It's Alden Waverly. I survived. I survived and I made it to the transmitter here at the Grass Camp. It's really me."

More silence.

"Where are your parents?" said the man.

"My folks were killed," said Alden, "but I survived. Mom was in the house, and Dad was blown up on the bridge, but I was in my cave. I survived. I made it."

Another pause.

"One moment," the man said.

The radio was silent for several minutes, then a woman's voice came on.

"This is Nancy Monmouth," she said. "Are you Alden Waverly?"

"Nancy!" Alden said. He knew Nancy. She was the head of the teachers and counselors when Alden's family went through off-world training for two years prior to their assignment on Cappa Terse.

"Alden, is that really you?" Nancy said.

"Yeah, it's me!" said Alden. "I made it."

"And you're really still on Cappa Terse?" said Nancy.

"I'm still here," said Alden. "Your ship missed me. I was sleeping in my cave."

"But you've been there all this time without supplies or a place to live."

"I figured it out. And I had help."

"From who?" Nancy said.

"One of the big animals here. An amazing buddy."

"But ... oh, never mind. Let's get you home. Can you stay at the camp there for another ten hours or so?"

"I've been here for two years," said Alden. "I don't think ten more hours is going to matter."

"We'll be there as soon as we can. I'm coming myself. It's so good to hear you, Alden. This is incredible. Hold tight and we'll be right there."

"OK, Nancy. See you soon. Thanks."

"My pleasure. This is amazing! See you soon, Alden."

"Over and out," Alden said.

"Closing com," said Nancy.

The sun had not quite set, but there wasn't anything for Alden to do except get some sleep. It was really weird talking to a person. It was so long since he'd spoken to anyone but Burly he nearly forgot how to listen to words and respond to another half of the conversation.

Alden finished off the last of his saved fruitleaves and

bottled water, and decided on a barracks to sleep in. With the corner blasted off of one and the front door ripped from the other, neither shut out the outdoors, but the bedroom doors were still intact. He chose the building missing the front door, since that one had the electricity running. There was no water supply, but enough left in the toilet tank for one flush, and Alden used it. That was a special treat.

Alden found a bed that was made—it felt the least like he was sleeping somewhere a person had just been—and lay down for the night. The bed was an astonishing feeling. Despite his workmanlike drive to get where he was, there were many nights he rested on his log, covered in shirts, and presumed he would never actually sleep in a bed again. It was heaven.

Morning came, and at the first rays of daybreak, Alden was up. Despite the bed, he slept poorly; not because of the change from being used to his log, but because of the anticipation. He'd missed the supply ship once. It probably couldn't happen again, since they knew where he was and were coming especially for him, but sleeping was not a comfy place for his mind to be.

The first thing he did was go call ECOP again, just to make sure he wasn't dreaming the night before. The supply ship was on its way, due to arrive in about an hour. Alden was only in bed for eight, so they were ahead of schedule. That was great.

There wasn't much to do to pass the time. He nosed around the big lab, but the main computer in there was blasted, and any research samples had long since shriveled up, so that was no fun. He wandered around outside, but wasn't interested in wading through any of the tall grass. That was a good way to get pinched by a crab, and the last thing he needed was an injury minutes before he was rescued. Looking at more things in the barracks just felt like an intrusion, though he did find a photo album and flipped through that. They'd shown Alden many of those, so it wasn't like he was prying into anything personal.

After an interminable wait and a couple of short walks up and down the buggy path out toward the plateau, he heard it.

Alden bolted back into the center of the Grass Camp buildings. He scanned the skies and saw the ship approaching from the east. It landed smoothly near the space between the barracks and supply shed. The hatch opened down, and Nancy Monmouth came running out to Alden. She gave him a tight hug.

"Alden, oh, Alden," she said. "It's really you." She broke the embrace and held his shoulders in her hands.

"Let me look at you," said Nancy. "Heaven's sakes, you're so big! You've grown."

Alden couldn't make sense of what he was feeling, but this was very strange to him. It was Nancy, all right, and the supply ship, and everything was how it was supposed to be. It just felt so odd to see a person. He suddenly had no idea how to act.

"How in the world did you make it?" Nancy said.

"I had a friend," said Alden.

"Yes, yes, you mentioned that. What kind of friend?"

"Burly," Alden said. "A burlon."

"A burlon?" said Nancy, incredulously. "You made friends with a burlon?"

"Yes. We built a bridge."

"Where is he now?" Nancy asked. Alden was no dope. He knew right away from Nancy's tone that she didn't believe him. He liked Nancy, but she clearly thought Alden was imagining things, or making them up. And Alden was not inclined to try to convince her. He knew what happened.

"He's ... back there. He couldn't make it."

"Well, let's go see," she said. She put an arm around Alden's shoulders and began guiding him toward the ship. "We have lots of food and drinks on board. What have you been eating?"

"Fruitleaves. And birds."

"Wow, you caught birds? I'd love to hear about that. Is there anything special you'd like to eat?"

"Cherry pie," said Alden.

"I love cherry pie," Nancy said, "but that's one we didn't bring with us, I'm afraid. We'll get you some first thing at ECOP. We have a change of clothes, for you, too. Good heavens, you need shoes." She pointed at his bark slipper. "You made that?"

"Yes," said Alden as he walked up to the hatch plank. At the top of it stood the supply ship pilot. Alden didn't recognize him.

"Gary, this is Alden Waverly," said Nancy as they ascended into the ship. "Alden, Gary Purefoy."

Gary extended his hand. "Alden, it's an honor to meet you. You are a very impressive young man."

Alden politely shook his hand. "Thank you, sir."

Gary had a few more comments, only slightly less condescending than Nancy's. They apparently either thought Alden was crazy, or that they had to be nauseatingly careful with him. Both felt a little insulting, but Alden wasn't sure why. He knew they meant the best; that wasn't it at all. It was just obvious they didn't know how to deal with Alden's situation. And how would they? Alden didn't really know how to deal with it, either. A whole new world was waiting for him now, and it was one he was going to have to learn, much as he learned how to survive on Cappa Terse.

And that is when my life began.

I accepted Nancy's offer of some snacks and a soft drink, which tasted like a miracle. I rejected her offer of changing my clothes, and sat at the window behind Gary's pilot seat, still with the pouch over one shoulder. I wasn't ready to be without that just yet. It would only fuel Nancy's concern that I wasn't quite right, but I didn't care.

As we lifted away, Gary kept the ship low and flew toward the plateau. On the way there, Nancy explained that our camps had been attacked by pirates. Marauders who took issue with ECOP expansion and went on a campaign to strike at our outposts. Not long after the incident on Cappa Terse, they raided a much larger settlement, one that was not defenseless. They were shot down.

I wasn't sure what to make of that. I know I was glad to hear it, but felt guilty at the satisfaction. I guess that's part of what being victimized is; besides the crime itself, it puts you in a position to feel bad no matter what happens. Weak if you forgive them, vengeful if you don't. I decided it was OK to just be happy they couldn't hurt anyone else, and leave it at that.

As we neared the ravine, Gary and Nancy became astonished at what they saw there. That was good, and I no longer felt like they weren't taking me seriously. They made comments and asked questions, but I don't remember what I told them.

I had a photo in my hand, from the album at the barracks. It was the blurry, far-away shot of a burlon. No way to know if it was Burly; probably not. I looked out the window at the scene and made my peace with it one more time. We were just close enough that I could read the wooden sign to the right of the grassland entrance, where the tip of the final plank rested. It had hand-painted letters on it, but the top word was scratched out with a deep gouge, and new letters were carved in the wood above it.

The sign said, "Burly Bridge."

www.ingramcontent.com/pod-product-compliance
Lightning Source LLC
Chambersburg PA
CBHW031946240626
47153CB00003B/879